Lara's Gift

Lara's Gift

ANNEMARIE O'BRIEN

Alfred A. Knopf
New York

THIS IS A BORZOI BOOK PUBLISHED BY ALFRED A. KNOPF

Grateful acknowledgment is made to the Overlook Press for permission to reprint five lines from "Autumn," four lines from "Cleopatra," two lines from "Winter Journey," and four lines from "Foreboding" from *Collected Narrative and Lyrical Poetry* by Alexander Pushkin, edited and translated by Walter Arndt. Translation copyright © 1984 by Walter Arndt. Published in 2002 by Ardis Publishers/The Overlook Press, Peter Mayer Publishers, Inc., New York, NY, overlookpress.com. All rights reserved.

Visit us on the Web! randomhouse.com/kids

Educators and librarians, for a variety of teaching tools, visit us at RHTeachersLibrarians.com

Library of Congress Cataloging-in-Publication Data
O'Brien, Annemarie.
Lara's gift / Annemarie O'Brien. — 1st ed.
p. cm.
Summary: In 1914 Russia, Lara is being groomed by her father to be the next kennel steward for the Count's borzoi dogs unless her mother bears a son, but her visions, although suppressed by her father, seem to suggest she has a special bond with the dogs.
ISBN 978-0-307-93174-0 (trade) — ISBN 978-0-375-97105-1 (lib. bdg.) — ISBN 978-0-307-97548-5 (ebook)
[1. Borzoi—Fiction. 2. Dogs—Fiction. 3. Fathers and daughters—Fiction. 4. Sex role—Fiction. 5. Visions—Fiction. 6. Family life—Russia—Fiction. 7. Russia—History—1904–1914—Fiction.] I. Title.
PZ7.O126713Lar 2013
[Fic]—dc23
2012034070

The text of this book is set in 12.5-point Adobe Caslon.

Printed in the United States of America

August 2013

10 9 8 7 6 5 4 3 2 1

First Edition

Random House Children's Books supports the First Amendment and celebrates the right to read.

For Aubrey and Anjuli

Contents

Ta-ra! Ta-ra! the bugles blow.
Up since dawn, the hunters sit
their horses chafing at the bit;
the borzoi tug the leash to go.
The master sallies out, surveys
the company: His easy grin
reflects a candid pleasure in
the little world that he purveys.
His Cossack jacket, patched and frayed,
is buttoned snug across his chest;
a brandy flask, a Turkish blade,
and horn equip him for the rest. . . .

It's dark, it's cold, it rains, it snows,
and wolves are on the prowl. But still
nothing daunts the hunter's will.
Up at dawn, he gallops off
to make his way, however rough,
through brake and brush, uphill and down. . . .

———

"COUNT NULIN" BY ALEXANDER PUSHKIN
TRANSLATED BY BETSY HULICK

Russia, 1910

On the eve my beloved Ryczar was born, under a bright full moon, the north wind whistled and howled. Like a forest spirit gone mad with merriment, it ripped through the Woronzova Kennel and sprawling grounds of Count Vorontsov's grand country estate. All night long, icy flakes of windswept snow drummed against the stable windows until the last pup was born at dawn.

Settled inside the birthing stall on fresh golden straw, Papa and I huddled around Zarya and her newborn pups—in awe of the wondrous miracle that lay before us on plush brown bear hides, for every borzoi birth was a gift from God.

"Lara, it's time to name the pups," Papa said. Whenever a new litter of pups was born, the Count gave me the honor of naming each one. His son, Alexander, told him I had a knack for choosing names the dogs lived up to.

With Zarya's permission I lifted the pup with a big red spot on her rump and looked her square in the face. "You shall be Umnitza. The firstborn is always clever."

Papa raised his bushy brows. Hidden behind the long black hairs of his beard, I glimpsed a grin full of pride. Like me, Papa was a firstborn, too. He gently tugged at the long, dark braid that hung down my back. With a nod of his head he motioned toward the rest of the pups. "We've no time to dawdle."

I put Umnitza down and picked up the second and third pups, both champagne in color. They had come out with such force and such quickness. "Your names will be easy," I told them. "You, little girl, will be called Sila for your strength, and you, sweet boy, will be Bistri, for your speed."

As I returned them to their mother, Papa interceded and took Bistri from my hands—turning him from front to back and front again. Then Papa ran his finger along Bistri's spine and grinned from ear to ear. "The Count will be pleased with this pup."

Like Papa, I, too, ran my finger along Bistri's spine. "But, *Tyatya*, I don't feel anything different."

"Be patient, Lara. You're only ten. You've got plenty of time to learn the art of breeding fine borzoi, so long as your mama doesn't give me a son in the meantime. . . ." Papa's voice trailed off into a sigh.

There was little chance of Mama giving Papa a son. She couldn't carry a baby longer than a few months. All of them had been taken away from us before we could even swaddle them.

I put Bistri down and picked up the fourth pup, as gold as the straw she lay on. She squiggled so much her tiny nails scratched me. "Such a sweet little thorn, you shall be called Zanoza."

"Hmmm." Papa eyed the little marks on my hands. "That name suits her well."

The fifth pup, of cream color, looked like he would grow up to be as fast as the north wind. "I will call you Borei."

Papa took him from my hands and ran his finger along his spine. "I'd wager my lucky hunting horn that this pup becomes the Count's finest hound one day."

Before I could run my finger along Borei's spine, a *swoosh* of wind clapped against the window and rattled the panes. I cupped my ears and listened to the ceaseless wind that clawed along the length of the stable walls in tipsy mirth.

"Your mama would say it's a sign and not a good one," Papa said. He shrugged his shoulders and gave me a look—the one that said I could pick another name for the pup.

He didn't believe in superstitions, and because of it, nor would I. "Borei's a perfect name for a top dog," I said with confidence.

Papa patted my head, like he would with one of the dogs. "That's my girl."

So pleased was I with Papa's praise, had I been born a dog, my tail would be wagging.

The sixth pup was the tiniest pup I ever did see and his coat was as white as snow. "You shall be Ryczar—my knight of knights."

I scooped him up and cradled him in my hands. Just as I nuzzled him to my neck, Papa grabbed him from me.

"Don't bother giving him a name," Papa said. "He'll need to be culled."

"But he's the only white pup in the litter." It was the color His Majesty Tsar Nicholas, ruler of all Russia, favored most of all. I was certain Ryczar would be prized more than the other pups—even if he was small.

"Zarya doesn't produce much milk. You know that," Papa said. "White pup or not, with the runt gone the other five will have a better chance."

Zarya's limited supply of milk was her only failing as a mother.

"*Tyatya, nyet—*"

"Enough." Papa's ruddy cheeks reddened a shade darker. "You know what must be done."

I did know. But knowing did not mean I agreed. As much as I dreamed of one day walking in Papa's boots to breed borzoi worthy of His Majesty Tsar Nicholas, I shunned culling any pup.

But what I thought didn't matter. Papa was the Count's kennel steward. Not I.

"Let me hold Ryczar one last time," I braved, for I knew what awaited the pup. A drowning in a deep bed of snow.

"You're only making it harder on yourself," Papa griped.

On tiptoes I reached up for the pup with outstretched arms, and a twinge of headache pulsed across my forehead. "Please, dear *Tyatya*. Just one last time."

"All right, all right," Papa said.

With a grumpy frown, Papa handed Ryczar back to me.

I smothered his soft, little rump with kisses and coddled him against my cheek. If only given a chance, this pudgy white ball of skin with knobby legs and a squished-in face might grow into a sleek, silky-coated borzoi with long, graceful legs, and an elegant muzzle to match. As I rubbed noses with Ryczar and took in the sweet smell of puppy breath, I counted my blessings that I had been born into a long line of kennel stewards and not into a family that harvested crops, for the borzoi wasn't just any dog. Borzoi were a national treasure, gifted among nobility like Fabergé eggs. A peasant girl like me might never get an opportunity to lay her eyes on a borzoi and I had dozens around me.

My twanging headache suddenly turned into throbbing pain at my temples. Quickly I put Ryczar down alongside his mother, Zarya. With my fingers pressed against my forehead, I tried to rub away the pain—a pain I had never experienced before.

"Larochka, are you all right?" Papa's voice carried a haunted tone.

"I'm scared, *Tyatya*." I pressed harder against my temples, yet the pain didn't subside.

I closed my eyes.

In the darkness behind my eyelids—as if in a dream— stood an older-looking Ryczar. He was smaller than most male borzoi and his coat was thick with wavy white curls. He held his head high and his chest puffed out with pride. Below him lay a dead wolf with silvery-red-tipped fur in blood-soaked snow.

Ryczar's image was as crisp as a photo and as real to me as my love for the dogs.

In complete awe and wonder, I willed myself to see more and squeezed my eyes shut until it hurt.

Despite my will, the image faded away along with the throbbing pain.

I opened my eyes and tugged at Papa's sleeve.

"We must keep this pup. I think I saw his future." The

words raced off my tongue like a borzoi in pursuit of its prey.

A hundred tiny lines creased Papa's forehead. "What do you mean?"

"Ryczar won't be the runt forever. He'll catch wolves just like borzoi are bred to do," I said.

Papa covered my mouth with his hand. "Not another word," he whispered.

"But—"

"Bad things will follow from a vision, if given credence." To scare me even more, Papa added, "You know how the Count feels about psychics like Rasputin. Do you want to lead a life like his?"

I shuddered at the thought. Whenever his name cropped up, harsh, ugly words flew through the air like a raging blizzard. "Of course not," I answered. "My place is here with you and the dogs."

"Then speak of this to no one," Papa said. "Not even to Alexander."

"Why, *Tyatya*? I don't understand." I shared everything about the dogs with Alexander. Nobody loved them more than we did.

Papa's ruddy cheeks paled and that scared me. Nothing ever shook his nerves. "Promise me."

Just then, Mama entered the birthing room, carrying our morning basket of black bread. With her black eyebrows, thick like a sable's tail, almond-shaped amber eyes, and pitch-dark plaited hair, I resembled Mama more than I did Papa. Unlike the stable clothing I wore, she was dressed in reds and golds and always looked like an iconic angel whenever she lighted prayer candles in the chapel.

No doubt for a second child.

"Promise what?" Mama looked from me to Papa.

"Evil courses through Lara's veins," Papa whispered.

Mama's eyes filled with worry. She knelt down beside me and placed the back of her hand on my forehead. "There's no fever," she said with relief in her voice. "What kind of evil do you speak of?"

"Lara had a vision," Papa answered, as if that one word would explain it all to Mama.

His stone-tight hands clutched my shoulders like a steel trap. He stared deeply into my eyes and looked like he had a thousand secrets hidden underneath his sheepskin hat. "If you have another one, you *must* ignore it, Lara."

I couldn't bear to disappoint Papa even if I didn't understand. "Forgive me. I'll never do it again. I promise."

"A promise is a promise," Papa stressed.

"Yes, *Tyatya*—Golden Rule Number One."

The lines on Papa's forehead softened. "To be a great kennel steward, you must live by your word, as well as by the Rules that govern us."

"When the Rules make sense, dear husband."

Mama and Papa exchanged looks that puzzled me. I didn't dare interrupt.

"Visions, whatever they might bring, are a gift from God—a gift we must embrace." Mama folded her arms. "Don't go filling our daughter's head with your nonsense."

Papa shook his head. "Only a fool in the guise of a devil makes decisions based on a vision." He grabbed his sheepskin coat and laced his felt boots. "I don't have time to bicker. I've got to ring the stable bells to announce the birth."

Papa snatched Ryczar from his littermates by the scruff of his neck, dropped him into an empty sack, and tied it shut with some hemp.

"*Tyatya*, let *me* care for the little white pup," I proposed.

"You'll be awake all night for weeks until he's big enough to eat on his own," Papa said. "Assuming he makes it past the first few days."

"There's nothing wrong with him," I insisted. "He's small, that's all."

"I don't have extra kopecks to bottle-feed every runt," Papa barked.

"I'll take on more kennel chores to earn his keep."

"Splendid," Papa said, crossing his arms. "Like you have time to spare. You already spend every waking moment working in the kennel."

"*Please,*" I begged.

Mama placed her hand on Papa's shoulder. "What harm is there in letting Lara try, dear husband? If the runt is not meant to live, as you say, surely he will die, regardless of her efforts. Give her the chance to learn this for herself."

Papa twisted the long black hairs of his beard, just as he always did when he struggled with a decision.

"This isn't the lesson I intended to teach you," Papa grunted, handing me the sack. "But your mama's right that you'll learn this for yourself, if you experience it first-hand. Your runt can have one final feeding with Zarya, and then his fate falls on you."

"*Spasibo!*" I thought I'd jump out of myself, I was so thankful.

"Don't come crying to me when the pup drops dead. Culling him now would save us all a lot of trouble," Papa said.

I unfastened the hemp and freed Ryczar as quickly as a dog licks his bowl clean. I wrapped my hands around him, brought him to my lips, and kissed his little face. And then I hurried him back to the warmth of his litter and placed him on one of Zarya's nipples. "Drink up, little boy. It'll be goat's milk after this."

Ryczar squirmed into place between his littermates Sila and Bistri and suckled. Gently, I stroked his back. "You'll remain Ryczar, for the knight you'll one day become, but I'll call you Zar in honor of your mother, Zarya, for bringing you into this world—and to me."

"*Korotyshka* would be a better name for the runt he'll always be," Papa said.

"Pay him no heed." Mama lovingly poked Papa's round belly.

Although he swatted at her hand, a slight smile crept onto his face.

"It doesn't matter what Papa thinks right now," I told Zar. "One day he'll see that it was right to let you live."

The wind whistled in beautiful song, as if it heard me and echoed after it.

"Curse that wind," Papa complained. He gathered three birch logs and tossed them into the wood-burning stove. With a poker he pushed the logs into place until they popped and hissed and a red-orange flame roared around them. Then he wagged his finger at me. "Remember, Lara. Not a word of your vision to anyone."

Even though it would kill me to keep it from Alexander, I answered, "Of course not. I wouldn't dare break my promise."

With a pleased look on his face, Papa left to ring the bells.

"Be careful what you promise," Mama said to me. She peeled away the cloth towel covering the black bread. From it she cut a thick slice, slathered butter on it, and then handed it to me. "Eat, *dorogusha*. You'll need your strength to prove your papa wrong about Zar and to help him find the truth."

"What truth?" I asked.

Mama took a deep breath. "The truth behind your visions. He's afraid of them."

Afraid? Papa didn't fear anything.

"Don't you see?" Mama's face brightened with hope. "God has chosen you. Accept his gift and learn to trust it."

As the *zvon* of stable bells, decorated in legendary borzoi images, clanged—*ding ding dong, ding ding dong*—the inside of my head felt like two mismatched pieces of a jigsaw puzzle.

Mama held one piece called Gift, and Papa held the other called Evil.

Neither piece interlocked with the other.

"I'm confused, *Matushka*. None of this makes sense," I said.

"Patience, *dorogusha*. One day it'll become clear to you which path to take."

While the crackling fire warmed my back, I peered down at Zarya and stroked her fine, lean head. Everything about it was pure borzoi, down to her long, straight nose, her dark, almond-shaped eyes, and her well-placed ears—tucked and hidden among soft, wavy curls. And just as Zarya had inherited these traits from a long borzoi ancestry, Zar would inherit them, too, as well as beauty and grace, speed and strength, and a keen eye to hunt.

A life without these splendid dogs I could not bear. Nor could I imagine living my life any differently than the way Papa lived his. Just as Grandfather had once served as the kennel steward for the late Count Roman Vorontsov, and just as Papa now served the current Count Vorontsov, I would one day serve as kennel steward to Alexander when he became the next Count. I'd be the first girl in my family to become kennel steward.

I would never risk losing that.

It became clear which path I had to choose.

I must keep my promise to Papa and get rid of the evil inside of me.

Suddenly the wind died down and the tug-of-war battle in my head ended. It became eerily quiet, as if . . . God had heard me.

Mama placed her hand on my shoulder. "It's a sign, Larochka."

I pushed that notion away. I couldn't let myself get sucked in by Mama's silly signs.

CHAPTER ONE

The Hunting Horn

Four Years Later
Russia, 1914

Like the moon, far from my reach, Papa's hunting horn hung high up on the tack wall in the stable, just above the birch-bark scroll inscribed with the Eight Golden Rules for breeding borzoi. Still, I could imagine holding the horn in my hands with its decorative gold pieces along the side. My favorite image was one of a borzoi running. It reminded me of Zar.

I could also imagine putting the horn to my lips, taking a deep breath, and blowing through it to signal the start of a hunt. Just as Papa always did, right before the hunters set off into the woods and open fields, led by

Kyrgyz stallions dragging long, open sledges filled with dogs and hunters.

More than anything, Papa cherished his hunting horn and forbade anyone to touch it—including me, for it wasn't just any horn. It had been in our family for generations—passed down from one kennel steward to the next.

"One day that horn will be mine," I said to Zar, patting him on the head.

"Not if our prayers are answered." Papa stepped into the tack room, with the Count's Gold Medal team of borzoi—Borei, Bistri, and Sila—prancing at his heels. The Woronzova trio were the strongest and swiftest hunting dogs on the estate.

"But you've been grooming me to take over."

Papa twisted the long, dark hairs of his beard. "It's clear you love the dogs. And it's true I've been grooming you to become the next kennel steward. All of that will have to change, if your mama gives birth to a boy. Trust me, Lara, I'm thinking of your future."

Up until now, I had never thought Papa would really take away my dream.

He turned away from me to dote on his favorite dog. While he checked Borei's paws for cracks, I tried to muster up my most respectful voice.

Instead, frustration poured out. "Everything I've learned will be wasted."

Papa gave me a look—the one that said I'd better watch myself. "Nothing is ever wasted. Your training will come to good use—as nursemaid—when your mama gives birth."

I glanced down at Zar in horror and mouthed, *Nursemaid!*

Zar nudged my hand and leaned his long, thin body against me. His touch usually brought me comfort, but my rattled nerves spread, like weeds in an untended garden.

"What if Mama doesn't give you a son?" I shouldn't have said such a thing aloud. In Mama's mind, just uttering the mere words could summon the evil house spirits, and take the baby away.

Papa quickly stood up and folded his arms across his chest. "Is that what you want?"

"Son or not—my place is with you and the dogs," I said. "To one day support Alexander when he becomes Count."

"Your place is with a husband," Papa snapped. "How will I ever find you a good one smelling like a pack of dogs, even noble borzoi worthy of the Tsar?"

Papa's words bit me like a rabid dog. He might have been thinking about my future. All I could think about was what a huge disappointment I must have been when I was born. No wonder Mama prayed at home and in the chapel as much as she did. She had failed Papa at her duty of bearing him a son.

"I know more about raising borzoi than I do about being a nursemaid." My voice quavered, but I wouldn't let myself quit. "I've cared for the dogs through distemper, tended to their wounds, administered their worming treatments, fed them proper diets, exercised them, whelped litters, and managed their mating, as well as anyone, even Alexander." I paused and caught my breath. Like me, Alexander adored the dogs. So much so, he deemed no kennel chore—not even shoveling dog dung—beneath his noble title.

"And most of all," I added, "the dogs listen to me."

I climbed onto the bench just underneath Papa's horn and pointed to the scroll upon which the Eight Golden Rules were inscribed. "Don't forget, I live by these Rules, too." Although I couldn't read, my memory was as sharp as the tip of a sickle. I pointed at the scroll, met Papa's eyes, and recited each Rule aloud.

Except for the unspoken Rule.

Golden Rule Number Eight was kept a secret among kennel stewards.

I had tried many times to pry it out of Papa but with little luck.

The Eight Golden Rules
1—A promise is a promise.
2—Hope for the best, prepare for the worst.
3—Never walk away from a borzoi giving birth.

4—Trust, but verify.
5—Mothers know best.
6—Three borzoi make up a hunting team.
7—An inexperienced borzoi is a dead one.
8—Revealed upon induction to kennel steward.

When I was done reciting the Rules, a half smile emerged on Papa's face. "Your spunk reminds me of me when I was your age."

"*Please, Tyatya.* I don't want a husband." I hopped down from the bench. "The only thing that matters to me is you, the dogs, and one day becoming the best kennel steward for Alexander."

Zar's feet danced as he circled around me.

"To breed true hunting dogs, you need hunting expertise, of which you don't have." Papa scooped a dollop of herbal balm and rubbed it into Borei's pads.

"Mama said you could teach me to hunt when I turned fourteen," I said.

"That's her promise, not mine." Papa pushed the wisps of hair off my face. "You need to learn some other skills—skills that will help me find you a husband."

Papa was right about one thing. I wouldn't make a very good kennel steward without hunting experience.

Sure, I'd hunted hare and other small animals with Zar, but nothing as big as a wolf. And really, what had I contributed? Zar had done all the work. And watching the younger borzoi train on muzzled wolves our hunters had caught, caged, and brought back alive to practice on—well, that couldn't be called *real* hunting, either. That was a mock hunt in enclosed pens, protected behind tall fences, with teams of borzoi and knives at the ready. What kind of skill lies in that?

None.

To breed borzoi worthy of His Majesty Tsar Nicholas, I would need to go on a *real* wolf hunt. But even that wouldn't be enough for Papa. To prove myself to him—and I shuddered at the thought—I would need to kill a wolf.

I had never killed a living thing before.

And wasn't even sure I could.

But I had to try.

With my shoulders back, my chin up, and Zar at my side, I harnessed my most serious, grown-up voice. "*Tyatya*, now that I'm fourteen, take me on a wolf hunt. Teach me what I need to know."

Zar pawed at my leg and goosed me with his long snout. "Zar's ready, too."

"Hunting's a man's world." Papa extended an outstretched arm over Borei, Bistri, and Sila. "With fine, fast, powerful dogs like these three."

"Zar's likely to be just as fine, if given the chance," I said. "Don't forget that Borei, Bistri, and Sila are his littermates."

Papa shook his head. "Look at him! Zar is and will always be just a runt."

At the mention of his name, Zar gazed up at Papa with trusting eyes.

"Zar might be small, but he compensates for it in quickness, agility, and tenacity," I said in Zar's defense. "You should see him zigzag after the wiliest of hares and pluck them from the air in mid-flight."

"Hares are one thing," Papa said. "Wolves are something different."

"Then train him. He deserves a chance," I said.

"*Nyet*," Papa said firmly.

"But—"

"Don't argue with me. Zar's no more suited to hunt than you are." And then he added, "Who hunts and who doesn't is a Golden Rule we must follow."

"There's no such Rule, *Tyatya*." And then it dawned on me. Had Papa let the secret behind Golden Rule Number Eight slip?

"There is now." Papa raised one finger high in the air, as if he were the Tsar. "By the power vested in me by my forefathers, I hereby declare—Golden Rule Number Nine: Hunting's a man's sport."

"If Catherine the Great—Empress of all Russia— could hunt, surely a young, hardy peasant girl like me could hunt, too!"

Papa's bushy brows bunched up. He handed me a basket and a small knife. "The only hunting you'll get to do is for mushrooms. Now hurry along."

Before Papa could impose another Rule, I obeyed, like a well-trained dog, and took the basket from him—wishing I could add my own Rules.

I'd make one that made sense.

Still, I carried a thread of hope—what if Mama gave birth to a baby girl?

Papa would have to bend, right?

I could hardly call Papa's order a hardship. The thought of fresh, meaty mushrooms, cooked in butter with onions, smothered in sour cream, made it all worthwhile. After last night's rain, mushrooms would be popping up all over the forest.

"*Davai!*" Zar and I headed through the main animal hospital that connected the dog kennel to the horse stable, through a long brick building, where the Count housed a fine collection of horses. Like each borzoi, every Orlov Trotter was assigned two trainers and a special team of animal doctors—well, except Zar. All he got was me.

"Where are you off to in such a hurry so early in the morning?" Alexei asked. Just like his Trotters, the Count's stable steward had a mane of long, thick, gray-white hair, and was equally important to the Count as Papa was on the estate.

"Hunting for mushrooms," I answered, trying to make it sound more significant than it actually was.

"Fetch me a good horse for Lara," Alexei said to one of his stable hands.

He chose an old dappled mare with a sagging back nicknamed Babushka because of all the foals and fillies she had mothered. "She may be old, but she's sure-footed and doesn't spook easily," the stable hand said.

Like a horse who's made the trip a hundred times, Babushka trotted by the racetrack and show ring, past the greenhouses flourishing with lemons, berries, and rare roses, and past the shallow ponds that cascaded down to the river, then through the fields in the direction of the forest of aspens, spruces, and birches. As Zar followed, loping, by our side, I inhaled deep breaths of the last bits of crisp, cool autumn air, for the harsh winter months would soon be upon us. The autumn landscape of purplish golds reminded me of Mama's favorite poem by Pushkin. His words hummed in my head:

> *The forest all in gold and purple clad;*
> *The wind-sough's whisper in the treetops breezing,*
> *The brooding sky with swirling vapor sad,*
> *The virgin frost, the sun's infrequent glinting,*
> *And hoary winter's distant ominous hinting.*

Babushka stopped under the shady recess of a cluster of tall birch trees sprinkled among spruces. She pulled the reins free from my hands and started to graze.

"This spot looks good." I dismounted and began my search for a sturdy, long stick. When I stooped down to pick up a spruce branch, I met Zar's kind, dark eyes, peering down at me across his long nose. In a squatted position, Zar towered over me and made me feel more like his pup than his guardian.

"How's this stick, boy?"

After Zar licked my face in approval, I ran my fingers, squeezing them along the rough edge of the branch, until the dried-up spruce needles sprang off like little arrows. Zar's ears perked upright. Anything that moved caught his attention.

"Such a true sight hound," I said to him. "If only Papa would notice."

Under my care, Zar had grown to be much taller than anyone had expected for a runt, and was big on heart. His most endearing quality was his loyalty—to me, for he slept under my bench near the stove at night and helped me with kennel chores during the day. Somehow I suspected he understood what his fate might have been, for he *never* left my side, unless he was chasing a hare.

Despite my endless begging, Papa never took Zar on a wolf hunt. "Zar would be as useful out on a hunt as Countess Vorontsova's lapdog," Papa liked to tell me whenever I brought it up.

His response always planted me right back in that very first vision of Zar standing over a dead wolf of silvery-red-tipped color—a vision that had not yet come true. A vision that gnawed at me—like a dog chewing on a meatless bone.

Papa refused to validate any of the hare Zar had caught over the years. "Luck," Papa had called it. But I knew it wasn't luck.

While I poked and prodded the rich earth with my stick through the damp moss and rotting leaves, Zar patiently watched. When I found the first meaty, dark-capped mushroom with a plump, creamy-white leg, I cut it at its base and held it high for Zar to see. And even though borzoi are sight hounds and hunt based on their keen eyesight, I let him sniff it. "Go find some more, boy."

With his nose to the ground, Zar moved through the wet undergrowth in search of mushrooms.

Suddenly the back of my eyelids started to twinge.

Oh, no! Not another vision.

Although I had tried to get rid of my visions, as Papa had insisted, they still managed to find a way into my head. In the beginning, they had come to me infrequently, never with warning, and always connected to the borzoi. The older I got, the more frequently they came. The dark ones were the ones I feared most and tried to purge from my thoughts, lying to myself that nothing bad would happen if I just ignored them.

But my visions always came true—except for the first one.

Countless times I had watched bad things happen when I could have done something to prevent them. I had started to question if I could sit still and do nothing.

Until we lost Zanoza, Zar's sister.

Because of the hunting success Papa had with Borei, Bistri, and Sila, he was eager to train their littermate Zanoza with one of the wolves he had caught and penned for such purposes. Papa was convinced Zanoza would be a star. The night before she was scheduled to go in a wolf pen, I had a vision of a wolf ripping her throat open. Like the sweet little lamb she was, she never fought back.

The next day when my vision came true, I rushed out of the training ring, sick as I'd never been, and threw up in an empty stall.

I swore I would never let anything bad happen again and that was when I decided to act on my visions—without Papa finding out.

To think I could have saved Zanoza had I spoken.

I might have failed Papa many times for not preventing my visions.

But I never once broke my promise to him, for I learned to keep them to myself.

The twinge grew more painful, beating along my

forehead, like pelting ice flakes. I closed my eyes, afraid of what might come.

And there was Zar.

He stood on his hind legs—battling a large silvery-red-tipped wolf with yellow eyes.

Gospodi!

I willed myself to see more. I had to know that Zar would be all right.

Like all the other visions I had had over the years, it disappeared as quickly as it had come and it left me shaking.

I searched into the distance across the open fields and found nothing alarming. So why did my gut still feel wrenched up in a knot?

I quickly glanced over at Zar, under the tall birches, nosing the ground for mushrooms, and then at Babushka grazing peacefully under a cloudless blue sky. The quiet alone could have swallowed us whole and the air felt empty, like the last bits of summer had been swept away with a broom.

Part of me willed it to be just that—another lazy autumn morning. I wasn't ready to take on a wolf. Not this wolf, at least. He was much bigger than Zar, and the way he lunged for Zar's neck with snapping jaws frightened me.

Zar pawed at my leg. In his mouth he held a mushroom gingerly between his front teeth.

"Molodietz!" I took the mushroom and dropped his prize in the basket.

He brought another, and then another.

"I'll never keep up." For every mushroom I collected, he found three, and he knew how to pick the good ones. Never once did he bring me a poisonous one.

The basket was half full when the pealing of stable bells sounded from the estate. The quick *ding-ding-ding* of the bells rang as a warning. I jumped up and scouted for something against the blue horizon.

"What could it be, Zar?" I feared the worst.

Zar's whole body tensed up, his ears stood on alert, and his eyes locked in on something in the distance, something I couldn't see. And then Zar shot off like a bullet.

I wanted it to be a hare that called him to the chase. But from the way Zar took off—with such intensity— I knew it was something he had never hunted before.

CHAPTER TWO

The Red Thief

"Don't leave me behind, Zar!" I rushed over to Babushka, gathered the reins, and pulled myself into the saddle. I squeezed my legs hard against Babushka's sides and clucked my tongue, until she fell into a quick canter. We followed Zar through the meadow, trampling through the tall grasses in our path.

Boom!

I flinched and looked around, wondering from where the shot had come, relieved that help was on its way. Babushka plowed on without a flicker of her ears or a stagger in her step. Zar, too, kept flying through the open field ahead of us, completely focused on whatever it was that had prompted the chase.

"*Gospodi!*" I cried.

A silvery-red-tipped wolf popped into view. It carried a leg of something white in its mouth—one of the Count's sheep, I was sure of it!

I wanted to scream: "Zar, watch out!"

But the words froze up inside of me like a river does in the dead of winter.

Zar gained on the wolf, leaped into the air, and caught it off guard—landing square on the wolf's back, causing it to tumble and scramble. In the blink of an eye, the wolf quickly recovered on all fours and growled at Zar with revenge in its eyes and bared fangs. Then it lunged straight for Zar's throat. Zar jumped up on his hind legs and thrust his chest forward to defend himself. Together the two stood on their back legs, fighting and butting against each other. Relentlessly, they pawed and growled and snapped.

Without thinking, I dismounted from Babushka and looked around for a stick or a rock among the tall grasses. All I found were pebbles and little mounds of dirt— which I grabbed and threw, grabbed and threw.

I was too far away to hit the wolf.

Boom!

The noise startled the silvery-red-tipped wolf just long enough for Zar to disentangle himself.

The hooves of a horse pounded the earth in a hurried gallop. Across the field came Alexander, riding an Orlov Trotter with his rifle pointed to the sky. Ahead of him were Borei, Bistri, and Sila, barreling forward with such swift force and determination.

By the time I turned back to the wolf, it was gone.

And so was Zar.

Borei, Bistri, and Sila reached me first, circling round me—their ears perked and eyes focused on the horizon for something to chase. Alexander rode up and pulled his white steed to a halt beside me.

"Zar took off after the wolf," I blurted. My lip trembled, but I resolved not to cry.

"You saw the wolves?" Alexander asked.

"*Wolves?* I only saw one wolf."

"They stole our sheep again." Alexander shaded his eyes with his hand. "Did you see which way they went?"

"My guess is that way," I said, pointing to the crushed grasses. "I've got to find Zar."

I climbed into the saddle and nudged Babushka into a gallop behind Alexander's horse.

"Ou-la-lou! Ta-ra! Ta-ra!" he shouted to the dogs.

We followed the trail of crushed grasses behind the trio of borzoi and came upon Zar and the wolves beyond the hill near the woods. With jaw-crushing bites, a silver wolf attacked the carcass of a dead sheep, while Zar held his own in a stare-down with the silvery-red wolf.

Bistri and Sila worked as a team and distracted the

silver wolf by nipping at its hind legs while Borei blind-sided it and pierced its throat with his powerful jaws. The silver wolf wailed as Borei clamped down. And in one violent shake, the wolf's neck snapped, and dangled from Borei's mouth.

Zar and the silvery-red wolf circled each other, waiting for the right moment to make the first move. When the smell of death hung in the air and the crying wails of the silver wolf stopped, the bigger wolf lunged for Zar's throat and caught hold. Zar let out a cry, yet wriggled free. The wolf pawed at its mouth and spit out chunks of white fur.

"Zar needs help!" I screamed.

Alexander raised his rifle and shot into the air.

Boom!

The wolf bolted into the woods.

Zar chased after him, until his legs buckled and he collapsed.

I began to dismount. "I've got to help Zar!"

"Let me finish off the silver wolf first. Your father will kill me if anything happens to you." Alexander pulled out his favorite knife—the one the Grand Duke Nicolai of the Perchino Kennel had gifted to him—and guardedly approached the silver wolf.

I closed my eyes.

"Molodietz!" Alexander praised the dogs when he was done.

When I garnered the courage to open my eyes, Alexander was wiping the knife's blade clean from the wolf's blood against his trousers. So I dismounted and hurried over to Zar.

I hugged and kissed and stroked him until I realized my hands were stained with fresh, wet blood.

"Zar's bleeding!"

Alexander rushed over to us and took a closer look at Zar's neck. "He just needs a few stitches. He'll be fine."

"I hope so," I said in a soft voice.

"Don't be so glum." Alexander pointed to the Count's Gold Medal trio of borzoi. "Zar's one of them now."

"You're right." Just then, an eerie feeling came over me, as if we were being watched. Although I didn't see the wolf that had gotten away, as hard as my eyes searched for it through the woods, my gut told me it was watching us.

And then a lonely howl pierced the air, confirming my suspicion.

"We should hurry," Alexander said. "Zar will still need some medical attention."

This was why Alexander and I were such good friends, despite my being four years his junior. The dogs always came first.

Alexander raised and lowered his hand to command Babushka to kneel. Then Alexander gave a quick nod to Zar. "Jump, boy."

"He's never been trained," I warned. In the absence of a sledge, injured dogs often rode atop horses to carry them home, as well as on longer hunts to keep their strength and endurance.

"He'll figure it out," Alexander said. "He's seen other dogs do it."

As if by instinct, Zar struggled to climb up onto Babushka's hindquarters. The more he dug his claws, the more Babushka whinnied, until she finally had had enough and bolted upright. Zar slid off of her and landed on his rump.

I moved to help him.

"Don't, Larochka," Alexander cautioned. "If Zar ever expects to go on a hunt, he must learn to do this for himself."

Alexander tightened his hold on Babushka's reins and repeated the hand signal. She snorted and pawed the ground with her hoof, before eventually obeying. "You can do it, Zar!"

This time, Zar took a few steps backward, and then in one leap, he landed square on Babushka's rump, carrying his head high. Once he was settled, Alexander raised his hand and Babushka stood up. With his fingers locked together, Alexander held them out for me as a human ladder. "Your turn."

"I, too, must do it by myself," I said.

Alexander smiled, gave me the reins, and stepped out

of the way. He then made a sweeping gesture with his hand, as if I were the Tsarina of all Russia. *"Pozhaluista."*

Under a blue sky Alexander and I rode side by side through the crushed grasses in the direction of the estate. Borei, Bistri, and Sila ran big circles around us, their heads held high, their eyes still searching for something to chase. Zar rested his head on my shoulder.

"I promised the French tutor I'd come back and finish my lessons," Alexander said. "I'd much rather help you stitch up Zar."

How I wished I could learn another language. "Say something in French."

"Like what?" he asked.

"Anything," I suggested. "Whatever comes to you."

"J'aime ces chiens plus que tout," he said.

Hearing Alexander speak French was magical like the moon, and just as far from the world I knew.

"J'aime ces chiens plus que tout," I repeated.

"Perfect," he said. "You have a good ear."

"What does it mean?" I asked.

"'I love these dogs more than anything,'" he answered.

I would definitely have to remember these words and repeated them in my head a couple of times. As I did so, I kept a lookout for the basket of mushrooms Zar and I had collected.

Alexander noticed it first and pointed. "Mushrooms?"

I nodded. "While you were studying French, I was

gathering mushrooms, until Zar noticed the wolf and stormed after it."

Like all the other visions I had had, I wanted to tell Alexander about my vision. Holding it inside was as difficult as keeping a borzoi tethered to a lead with a leaping hare in sight.

Alexander dismounted, collected the basket, and peered inside. His eyes grew big. "Wow, so many!"

He didn't look like either one of his parents, but, at the same time, he was a perfect blend of both of them. His mother gave him his kind blue eyes and his porcelain complexion. He got his height and slim frame from his father, along with his thick black hair that hung to his broad shoulders in wavy curls.

Alexander got back on his horse and tried to hand the basket of mushrooms to me.

"Keep them." I cringed at the thought of what might have happened to Zar had Alexander not come along when he did.

"*Nyet, nyet,* I can't," he said.

I knew he couldn't resist a dish prepared by the Count's head chef. "Marya will cook them just the way you like them, swimming in sour cream."

"Not fair! You know my weaknesses, Larochka," he teased. "But I'll accept on one condition." Alexander searched through his pockets, pulled out the hunting knife that the Grand Duke Nicolai had given to him, and put it in my hand. "Without your help I never would have caught up with the wolves."

"I can't take your prized knife, Sasha." I knew how much it meant to him and tried to give it back.

"I insist," he said. "You might need it one day."

Zar nudged my elbow from behind.

"Even Zar agrees with me," Alexander said.

There was no point in arguing. I was outnumbered. "I will cherish this gift, Sasha. *Spasibo.*"

The handle reminded me of Papa's horn. For it, too, had a decorative gold image of a borzoi running on it. "Look, Zar. It looks just like you."

When we got closer to the estate, Alexander took the hunting horn around his neck and blew into it to inform the stable hands that we had been victorious. Soon after, celebratory bells pealed. The *ding-dong-clang* of the stable bells made me feel important, like I was riding in a parade with the Imperial Family.

Boris, the Count's coachman, came running out to meet us, his arms pumped, cheering our success. "Did you get the ringleader?"

"*Nyet,* it got away," Alexander answered.

"There should be a price on that wolf's head," Boris said. "The neighboring estates have lost livestock, too."

"We'll get the Red Thief." Alexander said it like it was a promise.

For someone so big and gruff, with shoulders as big

as a barn door, Boris had a gentle touch with the horses. But trigger his angry side and he could break horseshoes and thick iron keys.

"We got the silver one," I said, praising Borei with strokes along his head.

"It's in the field just beyond the birches," Alexander added.

"I'll send someone for it right away," Boris said.

"Zar helped, too," I made a point to say.

"Zar?" Boris sounded surprised.

"I wish Papa could've seen him," I said with pride.

"His neck's a bloody mess." Boris looked to Alexander. "It can't be true."

"Of course it's true," I said with my hands at my hips. "Tell him, Alexander."

"Lara's right," Alexander said.

Boris looked down at Zar, then threw back his head and bellowed, "Don't try to make him into something he's not!"

"He just needs training," I said in Zar's defense.

"Then training he shall get," Alexander said.

Training was what I had always wanted for Zar. Now all I could think about was Zar gripped in the Red Thief's mouth.

CHAPTER THREE

A Candle of Hope

Thankfully, Zar didn't need the sick animal hospital, where we quarantined unhealthy animals until they passed on or, if they were lucky, pulled through and got cleared to rejoin the healthy ones. For practical reasons the main animal hospital connected the dog kennel and horse stable. All three sections of the stable smelled of turpentine from the rags we doused and hung from the ceiling to overpower the stench of the stools left by the dogs and horses.

I led Zar into an empty stall. And just like I'd done hundreds of times before, I gathered scissors, flax, a needle, and some herbal balm in preparation to stitch up a wounded dog—except this time the wounded dog was Zar.

"Be still, boy. It's going to hurt at first," I said to him.

I took a deep breath and punctured his skin with the

needle, drawing the flax underneath the skin on the other side, and poking through it. Zar cowered and winced. I hated seeing him in pain, yet pulled the two sides together and repeated the process three more times before closing off the opening. When I was done patching him up, Zar rested his head on my shoulder and licked my ears—giving them tiny bites of affection.

"Alexander was right. You'll be fine, boy," I said.

Zar's feet danced in place, from paw to paw.

Just then, Maxim, Papa's lead trainer, entered the hospital. He carried a sick wolf pup, bred from a pair of training wolves, in his arms. Maxim was twice Papa's age and kept himself lean like his wolves. "Is it true Zar almost got killed?"

"Hardly." I pointed to the four stitches. "Take a look for yourself."

"Hmmm . . . looks like Zar held his own," Maxim said, patting my back.

"I can't wait to tell Papa how fearless Zar was." To draw Papa's attention, I tied a long, white, cotton rag around Zar's neck.

At midday Mama was sound asleep, tucked under cotton bedding that barely covered her belly. At the head of her sleeping bench sat a sewing basket. I couldn't resist taking a peek. I pulled out Mama's work and admired the detailed embroidery and pearl beadwork along the lush, gold, silk fabric.

"I can see why the Countess boasts about Mama's work," I whispered to Zar. As I neatly folded and placed her work back into the basket, Zar retreated to his pallet just under my sleeping bench.

For luck I kissed the Mother with Child icon—which hung in the red corner decorated with vigil lights, eggs, dried flowers, and doves made of dough—not once but three times, just as Mama always did in times of hope.

Please, give us a baby girl.

So peaceful was Mama that I dared to rest my hand over her growing belly. Then I closed my eyes—longing to see a little sister inside.

As hard as I tried to summon my gift—all I could see were the backs of my eyelids, and they were as dark as black bread.

My gift never did come to me at will. The visions I had—always of the borzoi dogs, never of people—came to me at random, whether I wanted them to or not.

Mama suddenly jerked upright. She clutched her belly with both hands. "Did you feel that?" Her voice sang with hope. "The baby moved!"

I wanted to share her enthusiasm. With the baby so close to coming, the tension in our tiny, one-room home reminded me of a coiled-up snake ready to pounce. But I didn't feel a single movement, only the tightness of her big, round belly. Given Papa's order for Mama's bed rest, I was afraid to upset her with the truth and stared back at her with the blankest look I could muster.

"Don't be afraid, Larochka. I'm sure you'll feel it. Here, let me show you." She pushed the cotton bedding down to her knees, then took my hand and positioned it just below her belly button. "Now do you feel it?"

My hand flew from Mama's belly so fast, as if those little punches were on fire and would burn my fingertips. "Does it hurt?"

Mama laughed—a gentle but tired laugh. "There's discomfort . . . but movement is a good sign. I welcome each and every one."

Mama massaged her belly in big, wide circles. Suddenly her heart-shaped face bunched up in a frown.

"What's the matter, *Matushka?*" I took her hand into my own and squeezed.

"Your brother's restless and pushing against my back." She shut her eyes and began to rock. She hummed a few choruses of a lullaby, and then she paused to catch her breath. "He won't stop. He's going to be stubborn, just like your papa."

Every mention of the word *he* fed my heart bitter bites of poison.

Mama closed her eyes. In a soft soprano the words of the lullaby flowed off her tongue like the coos of a mourning dove.

Baby, baby, rock-a-bye
On the edge you mustn't lie
Or the little gray wolf will come
And nip you on the tum,
And tug you off into the wood
Underneath the willow root.

Mama sang this verse over and over. Each time the words became fainter and fainter until her weary voice faded into a tender hum. My eyelids had begun to feel heavy, as if weighed down by heaps of wet snow. Mama's singing soothed me, and I could almost feel her arms around me.

The only thing keeping me from a sound sleep was the thought of the Red Thief stealing *me* away into the deep, dark woods. Now that I was older, I heard the words to the lullaby much differently, for wolves, like the Red Thief, nipped and tugged for only one reason.

Hunger.

Mama rubbed her lower back with both hands. "My singing doesn't calm your brother the way it did with you. I'll have to find another way to ease his little soul."

If only I had been born a boy. Then Papa would have the son he wanted and would leave Mama alone.

It didn't work out the way Papa had wanted.

I glanced at the icon again.

Please, give us a little girl.

I prayed my prayers would be answered. I couldn't imagine a life without the dogs.

I was about to kiss the icon again when Papa entered through the front door, carrying a tray painted in flowery reds and golds against a shiny black background, courtesy of the Count's kitchen. Set within it was Mama's midday meal: a bowl of cabbage soup, a lump of buckwheat *kasha* slathered in butter, a glass of black *chai*, and a clay jug of honey to sweeten the porridge.

Papa scowled at Zar like he was rat poop in Mama's cabbage soup. "With the baby coming so close, we can't have Zar in the house anymore." He opened the door and ordered Zar outside.

Zar looked confused, but left.

"Tyatya, nyet!" I expected Papa to notice the bandage around Zar's neck, not kick him outside.

"Enough, Lara. You shouldn't be here, either. Your mama needs her rest for when the baby comes." Papa's voice was laced with genuine worry. Ever since Mama announced she was with child, he treated her like a delicate rose from Countess Vorontsova's greenhouse garden that no one was allowed to touch.

Not even me.

"No harm's come," Mama reassured him. "Lara got to feel the baby move."

Papa's goose-gray eyes brightened. He bent down on both knees and clutched the gold cross that hung around his neck, just like the one Mama wore. With his eyes on the icon, he kissed the pendant. "God pray this one's a healthy boy."

"He's a kicker just like his sister. That's worth more to me than a bag of gold rubles." It warmed my heart whenever Mama spoke of me, too—and not just of the baby.

"What's this?" Papa pointed to Mama's sewing basket.

Mama's face turned to one of guilt. "The work isn't strenuous, and it keeps my mind free from worry, dear husband."

Papa shook his head. "I thought we agreed. No more work until after the birth."

"I can't sit and do nothing," Mama said. "The Countess must be dressed in the very finest."

Before Mama's meal turned cold, I scraped the last of the honey from the clay jug and let it dribble off the wooden spoon into a thin golden stream over the *kasha*. With the honey I drew a silhouette of a borzoi running. Slowly the image melted away into the hot brown porridge. As I stirred to even out the sweet taste, vapors of steam rose and the scent of linden flowers wafted in the air.

"Mmmm . . . looks tasty!" Mama licked her lips, and then opened her mouth wide.

Papa grabbed the spoon from my hands and wagged it at me. "I'll take care of your mama. You've got chores to do and Zola needs your attention. The other dogs are stealing her food."

Papa surprised me. Ever since Zar took it upon himself to breed with Zola, Papa paid her less attention. He had wanted to breed her with Borei and she had refused him. So when Papa stepped away, I didn't stop Zar from mating with Zola. And just as I had seen it in a vision, Zola took to him right away. Papa was furious when he returned to see Zar mounted on Zola and complained that her litter wouldn't amount to much. Sometimes I wondered what Papa had against Zar. The way Papa ignored Zar seemed as if he went out of his way to do so, like Zar was some kind of threat.

Under a darkening, late-afternoon sky, I collected Zar, who had been patiently waiting for me outside the door. Along our way to the kennel we passed by the bell tower. Some of the church bells were centuries old, covered in motifs of icons and other saintly images. Underneath the bells stood the Count's official bell-ringer, cloaked in a priestly black robe, busy polishing and readying the bells for Sunday mass. Through the orchestrated peals and the clanging of the bells' clappers, field-workers easily followed mass during a busy harvest when every set of hands was needed.

"Our only hope is to light a prayer candle before it's too late," I said to Zar, and headed into the old wooden chapel. I hated to make Zola wait and resolved to give her extra meat to wipe away my guilt.

Hundreds of candles glowed against the gold-leaf background of the icons that covered the walls. I approached the Virgin Mary, bent down on both knees, and crossed my chest. A sea of candles, cradled in glass perched on iron stands, surrounded her. I lighted one more candle.

Please, I prayed, give me a baby sister.

Footsteps, heavy and hurried, came from the direction of the Count's private sitting room. With his hands at his hips in a smock covered in paint stood the artist the Count had commissioned to paint a mural of iconic images for his wife. His eyes were glued on Zar. "This must be a borzoi. Is it true they can catch a wolf? He looks so thin and small."

"Oh, yes." I glided my hand along Zar's side. "His brother, Borei, has pinned plenty of them. He's the Count's top dog."

The painter took a step closer, wiped his hand clean against his trousers, and then extended it to me. "Name's Ruslan Sergeyevich Savin."

"With pleasure." I shook his hand. "I'm the kennel steward's daughter, Lara Ivanovna Bogdanova."

Ruslan squatted in front of Zar and reached out to him, his palm up, for Zar to sniff. Playfully, Zar nudged Ruslan's hand, and then frisked around him with his front paws splayed, his head down, his rump in the air, and his tail carried low in the shape of a sickle.

"Zar likes you," I said.

Ruslan patted Zar on the head. "Such a regal dog. Look how much he resembles the Count, with his long, aristocratic nose. And the way he moves is with the grace of a ballerina dancing for the Tsar."

I nodded in full agreement and added, "A borzoi is to dogs what Pushkin is to poetry." I didn't need to know how to read to appreciate Pushkin. His rhythmic lyrics made it easy to memorize my favorite lines.

"That says something about borzoi," Ruslan said. "Pushkin lies at the soul of every Russian."

"Like your icons." My eyes wandered from one icon to the next. "Which ones are yours?"

"Nearly all of them. My specialty is faces."

"There must be hundreds."

Ruslan smiled. "One hundred and sixty-nine, to be exact. But I've never done a mural so grand in scale as this one." He pointed to the mural on the far wall. "I wanted to understand the way the natural light would fall on it. So here I am."

I took in the details of each face he had sketched out so far. What impressed me most were the eyes. They captured the emotional essence of each figure, such innocence in the child, such compassion in the mother. My eyes returned to the Virgin. Hers was the image I liked best. I could feel the motherly bond she had for the child in the expression Ruslan had created on her face. "The Countess will be pleased, of that I'm certain."

"Let's hope," he said. "Hers is a critical eye."

"I could never paint the way you do. I'm all thumbs," I said.

"With the right training you could be taught how to paint iconic images just like these," Ruslan said. "Of course, you'd have to cut off your braid," he added. "And wear trousers."

"Everything would be simpler if I were a boy," I said.

"Be careful what you wish for, especially for things that shall never be," Ruslan said. "We all have hardships we must bear. Artists, for one, never know where they'll find work. Most of us travel too much, moving from project to project, chapel to chapel, church to church . . . and we never spend much time with our families. Some of us don't even bother to start one. . . ."

His voice trailed off.

"I'd dislike anything that took me away from my family. That's why I want to become the next kennel steward, but my papa won't permit it if my mama gives birth to a baby boy." My voice rose with each word.

"Maybe this is God's way of steering you down a different path."

I sat a little taller. "The dogs are just what God intended for me. I know it, as I know my own name."

Zar lifted his head from the floor and let out a soft cry.

"Looks like Zar thinks so, too," Ruslan said.

"He knows so," I corrected. I reached into my pocket, touched the golden borzoi running across the handle of the knife Alexander had given to me, and carried my chin higher.

CHAPTER FOUR

The Red Door

I bid farewell to Ruslan and hurried to the kennel with Zar to tend to Zola. Along the way the cold, early-evening air slapped my face and the gray sky hinted of snow. Once inside the kennel, I couldn't help myself and ran from stall to stall, peering into each one, to greet every dog. "Hello, Borei! Hello, Taran! Hello, Buyan, Bistri, Buran, Lovkiy, Rossak, Ryss, Volan, and Vlast! Hello, sweet Zarya, Zvezda, Umnitza, Babochka, Bronya, Raduga, and Shaika! And hello to you, too, Dobraya, Skoraya, Snigurka, and Sila!"

In the last stall, where we kept our breeding dogs, I found Zola tucked in a corner, quietly resting on a bed of straw settled under the stone that hung from the ceiling to ward off evil spirits. Zar greeted Zola with eager little bites on the neck while the other dogs in her stall quickly surrounded me, nosing and nudging me for attention and pieces of meat. I put a lead on Zola and led her through the kennel into the birthing area. Zar followed beside her, his head held high like a protective rooster.

Zola explored all four corners of her birthing stall, sniffing and digging as she went, until she settled herself just underneath the stone that hung from the ceiling in a corner closest to the stove. Zar nestled up next to her.

"Such a smart girl." I curled up next to her and Zar, imagining what their pups would look like. Before I knew it, I was fast asleep.

Early the next morning Alexander woke me from a sound sleep. "Isn't it a bit too soon to put Zola in a birthing stall?"

"Papa said the other dogs were stealing her food," I said.

"Poor girl," Alexander said, stroking Zola's head, and then his eyes fell on the bandage I had tied around Zar's neck. "Is he all right after yesterday?"

"He's fine. I wanted Papa to notice him," I said. "Have you talked to him about giving Zar some training?"

"Not yet, Larochka." He patted his chest with both hands. "Up, Zar."

Alexander caught Zar's paws and waltzed him around the birthing stall. "Are you ready to become a father, boy?"

It pleased me that Alexander wasn't disappointed by the mating.

"That looks like splendid fun, Sasha. Zar's never jumped up and danced with me like that."

Alexander let go of Zar's paws. "Give it a whirl."

I patted my chest. "Up, boy."

Zar sat down.

I patted my chest again. "Zar, up."

He lifted his paw.

"He's afraid to hurt you," Alexander said.

"Please, Zar." I pounded my chest this time. "You won't hurt me. I'm strong enough."

Zar gently pawed at my leg.

"I can see in his eyes that he wants to obey," Alexander said.

My cheeks burned red from embarrassment. "He doesn't think I can do it."

Just then, Papa barged into the birthing area. "Your mama's about to give birth!"

"Hurry," Alexander said. "I'll watch over Zola."

Papa and I rushed home. Again, Zar was forbidden inside and curled up on his sleeping pallet, now positioned by the door. My knotted stomach waged a tug-of-war between my fear of Mama giving birth to a boy and my excitement at welcoming a sister into the world.

"The baby's coming. My water broke," Mama said between moans. With a strained face she kissed her cross three times. "Fetch the village midwife. Tell her the cow needs tending and offer her a payment that's customary, not a kopeck more."

"Tell her I'll give her an extra gold ruble if she delivers a healthy boy," Papa added.

"Remember to look for the red door," Mama said.

When I finally reached the village, where rows of log homes sat along the river's edge, women in dark dresses wearing colorful, flowery scarves over their heads were busy collecting buckets of water. Their small children toddled behind them in bare, muddy feet. I quickly found the log house with the red door situated on a prominent corner in the center of the village. I pushed open the gate made of woven twigs, walked past a patch of dying marigolds and a spotty garden of herbs, and knocked on the red door. A hawkish-looking man with clawlike hands opened it just a crack.

"What do you want?" He put no warmth in his voice.

"I'm looking for the midwife."

He forced a black, toothy smile on his face that looked as natural as a wolf cradling a lamb.

I stumbled backward in fear.

Zar suddenly stepped from behind me and stood between us.

A look of fright flashed across Hawkman's face and he slammed the door shut.

I approached the red door again and banged on it. "I've come for the midwife. Open up!"

An old woman with a hairy chin, bright red cheeks, and spectacles perched on a prominent nose opened the door. She wore her long gray hair in two thick braids that hung down her back and nearly swept the floor. "My nephew doesn't much like dogs. He's afraid of them," she said. "I am the midwife you seek. What can I do for you?"

"I came about our cow." I didn't like calling Mama a cow. But secrecy was necessary to ease her labor pains.

"The payment for receiving the baby?" the midwife asked.

"That which is customary," I answered. "Two loaves of bread—one rye, the other of sifted flour—a cotton shawl, and ten kopecks in cash. If the baby is born a healthy boy, my papa will add a gold ruble."

"Davai!" she said, shooing me out the door like a pesky flea. She collected a basket full of herbs and a small ax and was quick to lock the door behind her. From the window, I felt her nephew's eyes bearing down on me, like a hawk approaching its prey in a shallow glide before snatching it with a quick swipe of its talons.

"We must hurry," I said to the midwife.

For someone so old, the midwife moved nimbly along the path and through the woods up to the grassy grounds of the estate. The air had become suddenly much cooler and the late-morning sky had turned a steel-gray color that threatened an early and long winter.

"What happened to him?" the midwife asked, pointing to Zar's neck.

"A hunting injury," I answered.

She seemed puzzled by my response. "Does such a noble dog truly earn his keep?"

I thought it a silly question. "Of course he does. Why would you think otherwise?"

"Things of beauty can be deceiving," she said.

Zar was no doubt a handsome dog. For me, what existed inside of Zar was beyond beauty. Perhaps it was the bond that connected him to me and me to him—a bond I was certain would never break.

CHAPTER FIVE

The Birth

The moment we stepped inside our home, the midwife faced the family icon and genuflected. She put her basket down by Mama, lifted her bed dress, and peaked at Mama's private parts. I couldn't bear to watch and shut my eyes.

"How long has she been this way?" the midwife asked.

"Since early morning," Papa answered.

"I need to progress the birth," the midwife said.

"What can I do to help?" Papa asked.

The midwife pushed her glasses up to the bridge of her nose and eyed Papa with surprise. It wasn't common for a man to be present at a birth. "You're eager for a son, I suppose."

Papa nodded. "We've all prayed for a boy."

Not everyone, I thought.

The midwife turned to me. "You shouldn't be here, either."

"I need them both," Mama said. "She'll be married as soon as a suitable husband is found."

The midwife ogled me from head to toe, like a sack of beets at the market, and then turned to Papa. "My nephew would make a fine husband."

I gasped. "Our focus should be on Mama."

"Yes, of course," the midwife said. "Let's help your mama up from the sleeping bench."

Like obedient dogs, Papa and I pulled Mama up and supported her.

The midwife poked my arm and pointed between Mama's legs. "Crawl through three times."

I got down on my hands and knees and with my eyes closed scurried through Mama's legs, not liking it one bit—each time praying, *Please be a baby girl.* I worried something might drip down on me. And even worse—what if the baby came out and landed on top of me?

Each time I crawled through Mama's legs—back and forth, back and forth, back and forth—Mama moaned, "Tell me my baby's coming."

The midwife got down on her knees and looked again. A frown appeared on her face. "Your baby's a stubborn one. We'll have to hang you from the rafters." She pulled bands out from her basket and instructed Papa and me on how to attach them to the beams above, then she told Mama to twist the other end of the bands around her wrists and to hold on.

Mama hung by the beams, like a butchered pig, for several long hours, moaning and groaning.

I didn't envy Mama one bit.

By early evening, the moans and groans were coming one on top of the other and the bands had stretched so much that Mama no longer dangled in the air.

And then, at last, Mama announced, "The baby's here!"

"The head is starting to crown!" The midwife sprang up from her knees so fast her glasses fell off.

Papa took me in his arms and danced me around our long, whitewashed table. He looked like a young boy under the spell of his first crush.

The midwife moved Mama back to her bench and encouraged her to push.

And so did Papa. "Push, *dorogaya*, push!"

We all watched on—everyone praying for a son, everyone except for me. I was clutching Alexander's knife, wishing it had magical powers to deliver me a little sister.

———

Along with a loud wail, a strong stream of pee shot into the air when my baby brother entered the world. He was red and wrinkly with a puffy face. His arms and legs curled up like a bird's. Papa showered kisses all over Mama's face. She had finally given birth to a baby boy.

The midwife would get her extra gold ruble.

And I . . . I would lose the dogs.

For a second I couldn't breathe.

I felt like . . .

a bell-ringer turned deaf,

a borzoi gone blind,

a cook without a tongue,

and a painter without hands,

all jumbled together.

A small part of me also felt shame not to share in the joy. For Mama's sake I put on a cheery face. On the inside I pushed back tears.

The midwife took the small ax out from her basket and cut the umbilical cord. She tied it off with some flax. "To ensure his health is secure." The midwife paused. She took a deep breath and blew three times on the top of my brother's head. She blew three more times between his shoulder blades, and again three times on the soles of his feet before swaddling him and putting him in Mama's steady arms. Almost immediately, my brother stopped fussing and started to coo.

Papa's face unleashed such delight that a mighty jealousy chomped at my heart.

"Is he healthy?" Papa kept asking.

"He'll grow into a strong boy," the midwife answered each time.

With my brother in Mama's arms, Papa knelt down under the Mother with Child icon. "You've answered our prayers."

Papa's words numbed me like frostbite. My brother wasn't even an hour old and I already felt demoted from my position of firstborn in Papa's eyes. Tired of all the attention my brother was getting, I retreated outside and was greeted by the first snowfall. Zar stood up and shook off the flakes of snow that had gathered on his white coat. He arched his back in a long stretch, and then nosed my hand. I bent down and kissed his head. "We didn't get a little sister."

Zar licked my cheeks and gave my ears little bites of affection. So happy was he to see me, I didn't tell him what having a little brother might mean. It would wrinkle his heart.

Papa joined me outside. "Your mama's excited to name your brother. Come inside."

Mama looked down into her arms at my baby brother with such fondness. "We shall name our son Bohdan. He is our gift from God."

Their gift from God?

Why didn't they name me Bohdana when I was born? I wondered.

I glanced up at the icon. What happened to the little sister I had asked for?

Papa put his arm around me. "Your mama will need more help now that Bohdan has come."

"Of course, *Tyatya*."

"There'll be changes," he added.

"What kind of changes?" The firm way in which he said it alarmed me.

"The first few months are critical for your brother. We think it best that Zar stays in the kennel," Papa said.

"All right," I said. "I don't mind sleeping in the stalls with him."

"*Nyet,*" Papa said. "You'll need to be here to care for Bohdan."

"I won't be able to watch him and make gowns for the Countess," Mama added.

"What about the dogs?" I asked.

"It's time you take on a more suitable apprenticeship— one under your mama's guidance," Papa said.

Me—a dressmaker?

"But I'm all thumbs! Mama would have better luck teaching Zar."

"I was, once, all thumbs, too," Mama assured me.

"This is the best opportunity we have to attract a suitable husband," Papa said.

"He's right," Mama added.

My heart felt like it was being squeezed tight in both of their fists. I reached into my pocket and held Alexander's knife, wishing I had been born a son.

CHAPTER SIX

The Next Bride

For three days after Bohdan's birth the snow dropped nonstop. A white blanket covered the fields and meadows, as well as our garden. It looked peaceful, all still and dazzling white, like fresh sour cream spread over thin crepelike *blini*. So beautiful were the trees, cloaked in powdery white along their branches. I wanted to go outside and make snowmen with Zar like old times. How I longed to see him, Zola, and the other dogs. Instead, I had to prepare for Bohdan's baptism and the festivities that would follow.

With the midwife's help we cooked suckling pig and christening pudding while Mama busied herself hanging ancient coins and multicolored scraps of fabric as offerings to the family spirit to ward off evil and protect

Bohdan. In case those offerings weren't enough, Mama placed more candles, as many as she could fit, under the family icon and lighted them.

Mama spent the rest of the day cleaning Bohdan from his tiny toes and fingers to his itty-bitty ears. She patted him dry with our softest cotton rags, then dressed him in a white cotton baptismal gown that she had sewn herself. For the final touch, she combed the scruff of black hair that stood straight up from his head.

Papa summoned a priest from the village to perform the baptism. Alexander graciously accepted the honor to stand as Bohdan's godfather and I stood alongside him as my brother's godmother. Together Alexander and I held Bohdan while the Count's bell-ringer rang the church bells and the priest performed the baptismal rites inside the Count's chapel. Everyone fussed over Bohdan— touching his feet and pinching his chubby cheeks. Still, he managed to sleep through it all and hardly stirred. It was hard not to love Bohdan. Each day he cried less and less and even started to coo in my arms.

Once the ceremony ended, Mama and I rushed home before all the others and placed a sleepy Bohdan in his cradle. Papa arrived with our friends and well-wishers not long afterward. Mama stood vigil, rocking Bohdan's cradle, as Papa tended to each guest, offering them food and drinks. Alexei, bundled up in sheepskin, was the first to give Papa a hearty pat on the back, followed by Boris.

Plump-figured Marya brought tea cakes along with some of her kitchen staff. Ruslan filed in next with an icon of the Mother with Child and placed it in Mama's hands.

"Your thoughtfulness humbles me," Mama said to Ruslan. "We shall hang it over Bohdan's cradle."

On behalf of the Count and his wife, who were away in Moscow, attending the Imperial Ball, Alexander greeted Papa, and then presented Mama with a bag of gold rubles for Bohdan.

"*Spasibo,*" Mama said to Alexander.

Then he turned to me. "I've missed you at the kennel, Larochka."

"Me too. How are Zola and the other dogs?" I asked. "Has Zar's neck wound healed?"

"The dogs are fine and so is Zar's neck," Alexander said. "It's Zar's heart I'm worried about. He really misses you."

"I feel the same way, Sasha."

"Zar doesn't much like being cooped up in a stall," Alexander said.

"He's used to sleeping at my feet," I said. "It's good you've come. I thought you'd be at the Imperial Ball with your parents."

"My life is here," Alexander said.

"To see the Tsar—and his beautiful palace—would be like a fairy tale," I said.

"I'd prefer to meet the Tsar in a different setting, like

a hunt. I can't be bothered with balls, not when there's so much work needed to build this kennel. With you as my steward I will one day breed the perfect borzoi and host hunts like the ones at Perchino."

Hearing him talk about his goals stirred the dreams that lived inside of me. I wanted to tell Alexander that it would be Bohdan, not me, sharing in his big plans. Yet I couldn't bring myself to say the words.

Just then, Maxim barged through the door and announced, "Are you ready for Borei?"

Papa looked to the midwife for guidance.

"Let me gather the single girls." The midwife grabbed me first and stole me away from Alexander, and then she snagged the chambermaids, Darya and Tatyana, as well as the Vorontsovs' house servant, Olga, who had just arrived and had barely taken off her coat. The four of us had been good childhood friends and would have likely grown closer had I not chosen to work in the kennel.

As Papa wove his hand in the air like a magic wand, the midwife handed each of us a piece of the suckling pig's tail.

"Good luck, girls." Darya's smile faded into a lemony pout. "No matter how much I scrub my hands from cleaning the chamber pots, the dogs never want the meat I'm holding."

"Nor mine." Tatyana desperately smeared the piece of meat along her skirt.

"That leaves you or me," Olga said. "And I'm too old to lose again."

"If you want to win, make eye contact with Borei," I whispered.

"Why should I trust you?" Olga asked. "Surely, you want to win just as much as I do."

"I'd rather clean week-old chamber pots," I said.

"I don't believe you," Olga said.

"Time to disperse, girls," the midwife said to us.

I hurried back to Alexander. "You've got to hide me from Borei. I don't want to become the next bride."

"It's just a game," Alexander said.

"Not for me," I said. "The midwife is intent on marrying me off to her nephew!"

"At least you'd be close by," Alexander encouraged.

"Sasha, the midwife's nephew is afraid of dogs!"

"That wouldn't be a good match," Alexander said. "Follow me!"

We wormed a path through the guests to a crowded corner of my home where I triple-barricaded myself behind Darya, Tatyana, and Alexander. Unlike the hide-and-seek games we played as children, the outcome of this game could determine my future.

Olga copied my actions and hid in the opposite corner.

The midwife signaled Maxim to invite Borei. No sooner did he see Papa than he bounded over and nosed

Papa's hands for meat. When Papa showed him empty hands, Borei leaned against him and settled for a good rub. Papa showered him with praise and pats on the head.

"Bring us the next bride," Papa encouraged his favorite dog.

Borei wouldn't budge.

Our guests booed in a friendly manner.

"He's a sight hound, not a tracker," Papa said in Borei's defense.

The midwife whistled for Borei's attention and purposefully threw him a piece of suckling pig that landed near my feet. "There's more, boy. Go find it."

Borei trotted off in my direction.

"That's not fair," Olga shouted.

I kicked the meat away and it stopped just short of where Darya and Tatyana stood.

"This way!" Alexander led me to the opposite corner near the stove. "Hide behind me."

Borei poked and sniffed around the chambermaids.

Darya giggled with hope.

But Tatyana sighed when Borei snatched the piece of meat off the floor and moved on.

"That was close," I said.

Upon hearing my voice, Borei's ears perked up and he began searching for me. I tried to escape and rushed behind Olga.

"No, you don't," Olga said, fighting to stand behind me. "I see what you're doing. You want to win."

"I'm telling you. I don't want to win."

Olga refused to let me get behind her and left me exposed.

Borei's eyes locked on me—and when that happens, there's no escape from a borzoi.

"Olga's got a much bigger piece of meat," I whispered to Borei, who poked and prodded relentlessly at my hands. "Go to her!"

"Looks like we have a winner," Papa announced.

"Give him the meat," the midwife said to me. "He's earned it."

In one quick chomp Borei snatched it from my hands and searched for more.

I glanced over at Olga and shook my head. "It could have been you."

Mama was the first to clap. "Our next bride!"

But it was the midwife who clapped loudest. She had a mouthwatery look in her eyes, the kind hungry dogs get when they see fresh meat. While she reeled Papa in and held his ear, Marya tottered over to me and squeezed me until it hurt. "Let's hope your papa finds someone close by. You'll be sorely missed, if not."

Ruslan and Boris crowded around me, too, and patted my back. The two of them looked happy for me.

When my eyes fell on Alexander, his face was full of smiles, but his voice sounded like a rooster who had lost his crow. "Maybe you can teach the midwife's nephew to love the dogs as you do?"

"His fear of dogs isn't my only problem," I said. "Papa wants me to apprentice under Mama and become a dressmaker."

"*Nyet,*" Alexander cried. "He can't do that!"

"He has," I said. "You've got to promise me to watch over Zola and Zar and the other dogs."

"I will, Larochka."

"I know you will," I said.

"I still can't believe it," he said. "How will the kennel manage without you?"

"Sasha, the question is, how will I manage without the kennel?"

Days later, after the midwife tidied up from the festivities of the baptism, she whispered something in Mama's ear—eyeing me as she did so. Mama's head bobbed up and down, and by the way her face glowed, she seemed to hang on every word. When the midwife finished, she nodded to Papa, bid us luck, and left. Like every morning since Bohdan's birth, Papa kissed my baby brother on the nose and headed off to the kennel. Mama and I watched the midwife and Papa trudge through the snow in opposite directions.

"I need to get back to work, too," Mama said. "The Countess needs me."

"You should rest." I knew Papa wouldn't like Mama's idea.

"I can't sit still forever," Mama said. "My grandmother birthed my mama in the fields and continued working. To keep my coveted position on the estate, I mustn't give the Countess cause to dispose of me. Sometimes your dear papa can't see beyond his nose."

Mama didn't need to explain *that* to me. I had my own problems with Papa.

"We should start your apprenticeship while Bohdan's sleeping."

"Must we?" I asked in a deflated voice.

Mama put her arms around me. "I know it isn't easy to give up the dogs. But your papa's right that you'll need to learn a skill that's useful for marriage."

Hearing the word *marriage* tormented me in the same way as did watching a sick dog suffer a long and painful death.

I put Bohdan's *soska* back into his mouth to suck on, and then I checked his diaper and found a poopy mess. The smell was so dreadful I held my breath and quickly cleaned his plump bottom, wishing all the while we could hang turpentine rags above his cradle. I swaddled him in a clean cloth diaper and kissed his feet before bundling him up from head to toe.

With Bohdan cooing, snuggled up to my chest, we kept each other warm along our journey to Mama's sewing studio. Papa's footsteps had helped pack down the snow, forming a path for us. My eyes wandered toward the kennel and searched for some sign of the dogs.

"You must miss Zar," Mama said.

"You need me more than he does." Even though I resented Bohdan for taking what I cherished most away from me, it was hard not to love him. He was an easy baby and the littlest things made him happy.

Mama tenderly touched Bohdan's capped head. "For now, that's true."

The jingle of horses' bells, hundreds of soft timbres, filled the air. Mama and I turned around to see a gilded sleigh approaching, led by a troika of the Count's Orlov Trotters yoked together.

"The Countess must be returning from the Imperial Ball," Mama said.

Boris pulled up on the reins to stop the horses and nodded to Mama and me.

"What are you doing out in the cold and with the baby no less?" the Countess asked. She removed her hand from the inside of her muff and, in one grand sweep, she motioned for us to join her.

"It's really not necessary. We enjoy the fresh air," Mama said. "We've been cooped up for days."

"I insist," the Countess said. "Come join me for tea. I want to visit with your little one."

Once we were settled inside the sleigh, Boris clucked his tongue, and with a slight crack of his knout, he coaxed the white horses into a spirited trot. I pulled the thick bear-hide blanket over Bohdan to protect him from the brisk air. Heaven forbid he came down with a cold.

The Countess pinched Bohdan's cheeks. "My goodness, he's precious. How is he faring?"

"Bohdan's growing every day," Mama answered.

"Such a lovely name," the Countess said.

"And he coos like a bird. Listen," I said.

The Countess leaned in. "Indeed, he does!"

"Was the ball spectacular?" Mama asked.

"It becomes grander each year, with more and more exotic foods covering the tables, more toasts, and plenty of dancing until dawn. Nobody—excluding the Tsarina—was dressed as smartly as I."

Mama's face turned as red as a bowl of *borscht*.

To save Mama from turning redder, I blurted, "Alexander caught one of the wolves."

"Really? His father will be proud!" the Countess said. "Though I'd much prefer that he give up the dogs and give me some grandchildren."

We entered through the grand doors of the four-story

stone manor and were greeted by yips and yaps from Almaz, a fluffy white toy poodle—the one Papa thought would perform better on a hunt than Zar. The Countess picked him up to quiet him, and then excused herself to freshen up. The valet led us into the grand receiving room, where specimens from past hunts surrounded us. Covering the walls were the heads of aurochs, bear, lynx, wild boar, wolves, reindeer, stag, and heath cocks, all caught by former Counts. My favorite was a stuffed bear that Alexander had hunted, standing in the corner, holding a lamp in his raised paws.

Olga busied herself chirping over Bohdan. As she removed my coat, she whispered, "Next time, I'll make eye contact."

We both giggled, until the valet cleared his throat and glared at Olga.

Mama and I took our seats on a plush divan covered in a rich blue silk. We sat there staring at each other in silence, as some of the kitchen staff set up the samovar and asked after Bohdan in hushed whispers. They prepared cups of tea and brought in small cakes that filled the air with the sweet smell of honey.

While I held Bohdan, Mama fussed over him, smooching his splotchy red cheeks, and removed the layers of blankets that covered him. Then she smoothed out the wrinkles in my stable clothing and patted down the flyaway hairs around my forehead with her hands. She poked at the middle of my back. "Sit up straight."

I reached for one of the small cakes, but Mama gently touched my arm.

"Patience, *dorogaya*," Mama whispered to me. "It would be rude to drink and eat without our host."

How I wanted to taste one of the small cakes. "Just a nibble, *Matushka*?"

As if in prayer, Mama closed her eyes and had that look she made when she mustered up what little patience she had left.

"*Nyet,*" she answered quietly.

Bohdan was still asleep in my arms by the time the Countess reappeared. She hardly looked like she had just been outside covered from head to toe in fine sable. She came in through the parlor dressed in a red silk gown, her hair coiffed in bouncing blond ringlets. From her neck hung several strings of pearls and her floral perfume nearly drowned out the sweet honey smell of the small cakes. She held a string of small bells bound to a fancy band of leather.

"I heard all about Bohdan's baptism in a telegram from Alexander," the Countess said, handing Mama the band of tinkling baby bells. "I hope Bohdan enjoys them as much as my boys did."

"*Spasibo,*" Mama said.

"Well, well, well . . . Bohdan's a big baby," the Countess said as she took him from my arms. She rocked him in a loving manner, her gaze fully consumed on him. "I miss the days when Alexander was an infant. They seem so long ago. One moment they demand our full attention, and the next they no longer need us. All my Alexander ever dreams about are the perfect borzoi, the perfect hunt, and the perfect kennel. He has no interest in his father's business." The Countess turned to me. "You, too, should give up this nonsense with the dogs and follow in your mother's path. If you have half of her talent, I'll expect to see fine work from you. Perhaps you'll even sew gowns for Alexander's wife one day?"

I nodded out of respect and held my tongue.

"Surely you have a gift with your hands like your mother," the Countess said. "You should take time to develop it and not waste another moment with the dogs."

Mama cleared her throat. "Lara shall start an apprenticeship with me today."

"That's splendid news," the Countess said, careful not to wake Bohdan. "When your mama passes down the art, be sure to pay attention. I don't wish to be disappointed in the future."

I bowed my head for fear my face would reveal the truth—that I had no desire or talent to create dresses. At the same time, I wasn't completely foolish, either. If I couldn't be with the borzoi, the position of dressmaker was a much-coveted one, and certainly better than cleaning the chamber pots.

I felt trapped, like I'd been thrown into a training pen with hungry wolves, not at all sure the wolves were muzzled.

CHAPTER SEVEN

The Wedding Dress

Like a well-tuned clock, Bohdan began to stir and let out a cry. "He'll be hungry soon," Mama said.

"Don't let me keep you," the Countess said, pinching Bohdan's cheeks. "Boris will take you to the studio."

I wasn't ready to leave. We still had not had our tea and cakes. Everything revolved around Bohdan.

"Pity, we didn't have tea," the Countess said.

"Another time," Mama said.

My stomach growled.

"Good luck with the apprenticeship," the Countess said to me. "Remember, I'm expecting great things from you."

"I'm afraid I—"

"Now, now," the Countess interrupted. "You are your mother's daughter, aren't you?"

"Yes, Countess." I smiled and tried to sound convincing, yet it all felt fake.

And I kept thinking, I'm Papa's daughter, too.

By the time we got bundled up again, it was snowing. A thin layer of white covered Boris. He didn't seem bothered by it and looked as comfortable at the helm of his sleigh under all that snow as a baby tucked under a bedding of eiderdown.

I climbed up to the helm and brushed the snow off of his sheepskin coat and hat.

"Under a dry snow like this," Boris said, "it feels like an extra blanket of warmth."

I thought of Zar and how much he liked to play in the snow.

"The studio isn't far. I'd like to go by foot." I wanted to sneak a visit with Zar along the way, as well as check on Zola.

"My orders are to accompany both of you."

"It's me, Boris."

"I can't cross the line with such ease as you do. I know my place among nobility," Boris said. "Let me do my job. The Count and his family are kind and deserve my best."

"Forgive me, Boris. You're right."

Sometimes I forgot how different our circumstances

were from the others who worked for the Vorontsov family.

When we arrived just outside Mama's studio, we bid Boris farewell and trudged a short way through the powdery snow to the studio door. As soon as we entered, Mama rushed to nurse Bohdan, and I threw logs into the stove and listened to the fire crackle.

"*Matushka,* where do you get your dress designs?"

"Mostly from my dreams," Mama answered. "Sometimes the Countess shows me a picture of what she'd like."

"How do you manage to make so many exquisite dresses? I fear it would take me months to make just a simple frock."

"Some dresses take a week, and then there are some that take me years." Mama rubbed Bohdan's back to help him fall asleep.

"Is one dress really worth all that effort?" I asked.

"Absolutely." Mama cleared her throat and the words from Pushkin sang from her voice.

> *"An endless choice of rich attire;*
> *Now she will gleam with ruby fire,*
> *Now robed and cloaked in purple shades*
> *Aglow with dyes of Tyrian maids."*

They came from Pushkin's poem about Cleopatra. Mama had often recited it to me growing up while she did intricate beadwork on the dresses she made for the Countess.

"Pushkin's words inspired me to make you a dress worthy of Queen Cleopatra," Mama said. "A dress I've worked on for years. A dress that's not yet complete."

"My stable clothes suit me fine. Why would I need a dress, *Matushka*?" I asked in bewilderment.

"For your wedding day, *dorogusha*." Mama pointed to a rack of unfinished dresses. "It's hidden here. Come see for yourself."

I approached the rack and fingered dresses made from velvet and silk, organza and lace, as well as chiffon and satin. Each time I gazed upon a gown, I found myself more and more drawn to what it would be like to wear a fine dress made by Mama's hands.

It wasn't until my eyes fell upon a dress as white as Zar that I thought this must be the one. I took the dress off its hanger and held it up against my shoulders. Such fine lace and beaded pearls all over the bodice, and the way the gown flowed to the floor made my heart swoon.

"It's beautiful," I said with unleashed joy.

Mama glowed with pride.

"How could you afford it?" I had never worn silk

before and thought it much too splendid for a girl like me who spent most of her days in a kennel.

"I added beads and ribbons here and there as I could afford it," Mama said. She placed Bohdan on her other breast.

I noticed a subtle embroidered pattern of borzoi along the unfinished hem. "Oh, *Matushka*! The dogs are perfect."

"Try it on," she said.

I peeled off my shirt and slipped the fine dress over my head. With her free hand Mama pulled the laces together along the length of my back and tightened them. The dress felt like a cool bath on a hot and humid day. The sleeves fit snugly around the length of my arm and opened up at the elbow.

When I moved and twirled around, the silk overlay flowed in a graceful and elegant manner, much like that of a borzoi. Even when I was just a baby, Mama knew what would be important to me.

The bodice glimmered under the dim light and made a kennel girl like me feel like a girl of noble origin, born to be led around the ballroom, dipping and twirling under the candlelight of chandeliers.

"It feels as if your arms are wrapped around me, *Matushka*, holding me tightly."

"I hope that feeling never leaves you, Larochka."

Mama patted Bohdan's back until he burped, then

placed him in a big basket cushioned by blankets. She took my hands into her own, and then it suddenly dawned on me. "Has Papa found me a husband?"

The wedding dress Mama had sewn for me—regardless of all the love she had put into it—now sat as a heavy yoke upon my shoulders.

"Well, *dorogusha,* there is someone in the village that he's considering."

"Who, *Matushka?*"

"It seems the midwife has a nephew," Mama said. "A marriage to him would keep you close to home."

"You can't be serious, *Matushka.* He's afraid of dogs. How would we manage together?"

"You'll adapt, as I did, Lara, and the love will come. No man is perfect in the beginning."

My love was reserved for the dogs and the dogs alone. *J'aime ces chiens plus que tout.*

If only I still had my kennel chores to keep my mind off of a loveless marriage that would take me away from Alexander and the dogs, away from my family, and away from Zar.

"The midwife asked me what skills you had—and I didn't much like stretching the truth. Other suitors will inquire, too," Mama said.

"I have plenty of skills," I said. "Like nursing pups, tending sick dogs, and preparing food for all the borzoi."

"Those are hardly the kind of skills I'm talking about,"

Mama said. "Now that your brother's sleeping, why don't we start your apprenticeship?"

I pushed the idea of marriage to the midwife's nephew far from my thoughts and twirled around one last time. When I peeled the dress off, my eyes gravitated to the embroidered borzoi along the hem. "Let's start with embroidery."

Mama handed me some patterns and scraps of fabric.

I rifled through her designs and settled on a simple pattern of a rosette in bloom and a swatch of pink cotton. Mama threaded a needle and did a few practice stitches. "Like this—nice and easy."

The way Mama moved the needle and thread in and out of the fabric reminded me of a borzoi running through deep snow—popping in and out. "Follow the lines and keep your stitches consistent in length," she added.

The start of a headache pulsed across my forehead as I took the needle and thread from her. The more it pulsed, the harder I pierced the fabric.

"Not so hard, Lara. Gently."

Even with a pattern to guide me, my stitches varied in length. The more I kept stabbing myself with the needle, the more spitting mad I became. When I finished my rosette in bloom, it looked like a bunch of angry circles enclosed within a bigger one dotted by bloody fingerprints. I presented my work to Mama.

"Oh, dear." She looked at my fingertips and shook her head. "Lucky for you they'll heal."

Mama checked on Bohdan, then sat me down with some paper and a feather pen. "Let's try sketching dresses."

I took the pen and began to draw. Before I finished, I balled up the paper and tossed it into the pail filled with Mama's scraps. I took another sheet of paper, and then another, and another. All of them ended up in crumpled balls with Mama's scraps. Every dress I had drawn looked like a sack. None of my designs would have impressed the Countess, of that I was certain.

One by one Mama picked through my papers and flattened them out. "Don't be hard on yourself. It's difficult work. Try closing your eyes. Let the pen take you where it wants to go," Mama suggested.

I closed my eyes and loosened my grip on the pen. My hand moved with ease and a certain calm came to me.

"Let me have a look." Mama took the paper into her hands. "Is this what came to you—a borzoi?"

Just then, my temples pounded.

I pressed my fingers against the pain and closed my eyes.

There were Zola and Zar snuggled in the soft straw, coddling six pups. Or was it seven? The white pup—a female—faded in and out.

Something in the way the pup faded in and out made me worry.

"Larochka, are you all right?"

"I'm concerned about one of Zola's pups."

"Did she have them already?" Mama's voice sounded surprised.

"Well . . . um . . . no, I don't think so." I didn't know what to say and stopped.

Mama looked at me, puzzled. "You're scaring me, Lara. What's wrong?"

"It's nothing," I lied.

And then Mama's eyes grew big. "You had a vision, didn't you?"

The concern in her voice was like a magical key that broke down a door that I thought had been sealed shut. "I'm sick about it. I promised Papa I would get rid of them."

"Have you been having them all along?" Mama asked.

I nodded in shame.

"You should have told us. I thought they had stopped coming to you," Mama said. "Well, that changes everything in my mind. You must live the life that God has chosen for you. Your papa and I shall adjust to God's will."

"Adjust? If Papa finds out that I'm still having visions, he'll *never* let me near the dogs again. And I belong with them. It's what I know."

"That's becoming clear to me. I wish I had known,"

Mama said. She glanced down at my sketch of a borzoi. "You need to tell your papa."

"I can't, *Matushka*. I'm afraid," I said. "You saw how he reacted the first time I had a vision."

"Then you must find a way to prove him wrong."

"How?" I asked.

Mama's face bunched up in thought. "Trust in God. Through your gift he'll show you the way."

Just then, Bohdan fidgeted. His tiny lips opened and closed like a newborn pup rooting for milk.

"Who'll help you with Bohdan?"

"I'll make do." Mama picked up Bohdan, gently kissed his cheeks, and then prepared to nurse him. "I come from hardy stock, remember?"

With any luck her hardy stock lived in me, too. I would need it to prove Papa wrong.

CHAPTER EIGHT

The Bet

Just as I bundled up in my sheepskin coat and fur hat, eager to be reunited with the dogs, I heard scratching at the studio door. When I opened it, Zar bounded inside, circled me, and then leaned against my legs, looking up at me with happy eyes. I got down and hugged my arms around him, stroking and petting him, like it was the first time I ever saw a dog. I ran my fingers through his curls and checked the wound on his neck. And just like Alexander had said, it had healed.

"Zar's coming is a sign," Mama said.

The thought gave me strength.

"*Davai*, we must hurry and check on Zola," I said to him.

We raced outside through the deep snow in the direction of the kennel, past the wooden chapel and its bell tower. When we reached the kennel, we sped past the stalls lined with lounging borzoi. I found Zola tucked in the corner of the birthing stall where I had left her, quietly resting on a bed of straw. Zar bounded over to her and nibbled gently on her ears and along her neck. She rolled in closer to him and grunted.

Just as I settled next to Zola a slight headache formed, and then Papa barged into the birthing area. "I thought I saw you come in here. You should be helping your mama."

"She told me I could visit the dogs." I saw panic on Papa's face. "Don't worry, Bohdan's quite fine."

Papa ranted, but I didn't hear him. My head ached.

I quickly turned from Papa to hide my vision and closed my eyes with worry.

There was Zola giving birth to the pups!

And then the image faded.

"Tonight's the night," I blurted in excitement.

I quickly cupped my mouth, wishing I could take back the words.

"What's that supposed to mean?" Papa's voice sounded scared.

"Tonight, Zola will give birth."

"The pups aren't due for another week." Papa looked over at Zola resting peacefully in the fresh golden straw of the birthing stall. She lay flat on her side, her eyes closed. Her silky-coated chest, painted in golden hues against patches of white, rose and fell gently with each breath. "She's not showing any signs of labor, either. What makes you think the pups are coming tonight?"

I edged closer to Papa and rested my chin along the mahogany slabs of the stall. I could hardly blame him for his question. Normally Zola acted much more nervous right before a birth, panting and pacing.

But Zola was as calm as Zar.

Could I be wrong about the pups coming tonight?

In my wondering I could hear Mama's voice, *Trust, Lara, trust,* and I could see her heart-shaped face, framed by long, dark braids. It was her kind amber eyes I could see most. They were willing me to trust my gift, urging me to speak up.

Yet the words crawled off my tongue. "I . . . had . . . a . . . vision."

Papa's ruddy cheeks turned white. "Not another word! Do you hear?"

"I see things, *Tyatya*—I can't help it!"

"I told you to get rid of them." Papa wagged his meaty finger at me.

"I've tried, *Tyatya*."

"You didn't try hard enough," he said. "You've got to ignore them."

"Why should I ignore them, when they can help us?"

Papa harrumphed. "Mistakes are made from decisions based on visions. I can't let that happen."

"Have you ever wondered how I was always the first to inform you of a litter coming? Or when a pup became ill in the night and needed tending?" I asked. "And what about the time when Snigurka got lost chasing a hare? Do you remember who found her, *Tyatya*? Me."

"I've got to put my faith in the Rules. It's what I know."

The deeper Papa's words sunk into my thoughts, the more they poked at my heart. "When it comes to the dogs, put your faith in *me*—there will be six or seven pups born tonight. That's something your Rules can't tell you."

Papa's eyes brightened, as they always did whenever a big litter was born. The Count often rewarded him with a heap of gold rubles. Not to mention my favorites: black caviar served on silver platters, sour cream brimming from crystal bowls, stacks of warm *blini* wrapped in linen spun from silk, and stuffed suckling pig dressed in horseradish—a symbol of abundance and fertility. To wash it all down, the Count always pulled out his finest bottles of iced champagne for a proper toast.

"Shhh." Papa put his finger to his lips. He looked over his shoulder, and then he leaned into me, his face so close to mine.

"Do you want to live a life like Rasputin?"

As favored as Rasputin was with the Tsar and his wife,

Alexander's family feared Rasputin had too much influence over the Imperial Family. There were even threats on his life.

"A life like his would be awful."

Papa turned his attention to Zola. He twisted his long black beard, deep in thought. His gaze moved upward to the icon of the Mother with Child that hung above Zola for good luck. It had been hanging in that very spot for hundreds of years—for as long as my ancestors had been breeding borzoi for the Count and his family before him. Papa never stood idle for too long. Yet he studied that icon, as if the answer to all his questions hid behind the gold leaf of the painting.

"Zola shouldn't be left alone," I said.

Papa tried to ignore me. Quick to remind him about his own Rules, I added, "Golden Rule Number Three: Never walk away from a borzoi giving birth."

Papa threw his arms in the air. "Nobody's going to work overnight on a hunch, waiting for puppies that may or may not come."

"I will." It was time I prove Papa wrong about my gift.

"Your mama needs you, as does your brother," Papa said.

"Mama said she'd be fine."

Papa frowned and his gray eyes looked as cold as a winter storm.

"Mama understands me, *Tyatya*. I thought you did, too."

"This isn't the life I want for you." He tucked the loose strands of my hair behind my ears. As he put on his sheepskin coat, he cleared his throat, and raised one finger high into the air. "I don't think the pups will come tonight, and to prove *you* wrong, I'll let you stay with Zola. Just this once. If the pups don't come tonight, then you're to forget about the dogs and devote your full attention to helping your mama. Agreed?"

"And what if the pups come?"

Papa took another long, hard look at Zola resting peacefully in the straw. "The pups won't come tonight," he answered. "Of that I'm certain. Should a miracle occur, I'll gladly reveal the secret behind Golden Rule Number Eight."

Before he could change his mind, I snatched his hand and shook it, for as much as I had begged him in the past to tell me what hid behind Golden Rule Number Eight, I never could wrench it out of him.

"Are we done? I have work." Papa let go of my hand and as he hurried off, he turned to me, and almost as an afterthought, he added, "If the pups come tonight, you know where to find me."

A big smile came to my face. "Not *if, Tyatya, when*."

CHAPTER NINE

Chara

Outside, under a glowing full moon, the north wind whistled and beat against the stable windows, as swirls of snow tossed in the air like long fluttering ribbons—flying higher and higher until they faded into the inky darkness of the night sky. I quickly lost myself in the vanishing trails of windswept snow. If only the north wind could swoop up my baby brother and make *him* disappear.

I chastised myself for such a dreadful thought and prayed the spirits wouldn't come for little Bohdan.

"All right, Zar. Let's get ready." It was Zola's night, and I needed to make preparations. Golden Rule Number Two—Hope for the best, prepare for the worst.

I kindled the stove and stoked the fire, for the pups would need the extra warmth. Red-orange flames roared and a blast of hot air hit my face. I pulled out the medicine box and gathered clean cotton towels and some healing herbs. From deep inside my pocket I pulled out Alexander's knife and polished the metal blade until I could see my reflection, in case I had to cut an umbilical cord or pup's sac. Then I sorted through a pile of bear hides trimmed with black velvet, picking the fluffiest one to line the birthing nest. I took another for myself and laid it on the straw next to Zola.

Her dark eyes opened just a bit as she lifted her head, just long enough to take notice of the fuss I made, before letting it flop back down on the straw.

"You'll be okay, girl." Slowly, I glided my hand along her big belly in search of movement inside.

Nothing.

Who knew how long I would have to wait, but I didn't care as long as I remained united with Zar and the other borzoi. So I found a cozy position with Zar curled up next to me, pawing my pocket for meat.

"All gone." I let him see my empty hands as proof, for borzoi trusted no other sense more than their eyes.

Zar let out a soft moan and nudged my hand.

"Silly boy," I said. "If I had any meat, it would go to Zola. She's got the tough job ahead of her."

At the sound of her name, Zola stood and shook the strands of straw loose from her fur. A thin greenish discharge dripped from her buttocks. And like a caged, cooped-up wild animal, she paced—with commanding dignity—around the stall, panting.

Back and forth. Back and forth.

"The pups are coming!" I could hardly wait to see Papa's face when the first pup came out. I hugged Zar and fought every urge to kick up my feet and dance. I needed to stay calm. For Zola.

"When you're ready," I said to her, "so, too, shall be your birthing nest." I laid the thick, plush hide down on top of the straw she had burrowed, and then brushed the fur from side to side with my hands, imagining the newborn pups, nursing, cozy and warm, nestled between Zola's long legs.

I kissed the icon of the Mother with Child that hung on the wall above her. For extra luck I kissed it two more times.

"It's time to fetch Papa, Zar."

Bundled up as I was when we got outside, the cold night air seeped through the seams of my coat. With Zar by my side, I dashed by the wooden chapel flanked by its bell tower, and past the tall white birches that bordered the estate—slipping and sliding on the icy patches that dotted my path along my way home. Wind-driven pellets of snow stung my face like the cuts of a thousand tiny knives. It would all be worth it to see Papa's expression when I told him the news about the pups.

As I unlatched the door of our home, it flew open,

hurled by a gust of wind. I pushed against the heavy old slab of oak, and shut the door with a thrust of my hip. Careful not to wake Mama or Bohdan, I tiptoed over to Papa's sleeping bench and gently shook him. "Wake up, *Tyatya*," I whispered. "The pups are coming!"

Papa rose from his sleeping bench rubbing his eyes, his fur hat planted on the top of his head. "It can't be," he kept saying. Still, he gathered his coat and sat down to lace his felt boots. "I don't understand," he said. "Zola has another week yet. Are you sure?"

I put my hands on my hips. "You need to hurry, *Tyatya*. Zola's close."

"I'm hurrying. I'm hurrying."

By the time we raced back to the birthing stall, full out of breath, Zola was moving in nervous circles, confined within the walls of the birthing stall.

"I can't believe it." Papa's mouth hung agape. He placed his hunting horn around his neck for luck.

Zar took a cautious half step toward Zola and she growled. With his feathery tail between his legs, Zar scurried back to me and leaned against my legs, as he often did when he wanted a hug. "Sorry, boy. All we can do is wait."

Poor Zola. Even though she had experience giving birth, she paced about as if it were her first time, her eyes big and wide, like a frightened doe. And all that back and forth, back and forth, made my stomach queasy.

How I wished I could speed up the process.

"It's on nights like this that I remind myself how fortunate I am." Papa held his hunting horn close to his chest. "We nearly lost the borzoi breed sixty years ago when serfs, like my grandparents, were liberated from servitude to noble landowners, like the Vorontsovs, and abandoned the country estates for jobs in Moscow and St. Petersburg."

Whenever we waited for a litter, Papa often reminisced about the past.

"It's important that we never forget—that we do what's necessary to preserve the breed," Papa stressed again and again. "We almost lost the borzoi once from inbreeding and outcrossing with other breeds. We must never let it happen again."

I placed my hand on the knife—hidden in my pocket—that Alexander had given to me. "Thank God for the Grand Duke Nicolai, who stepped in and brought the borzoi back to its pure form."

"And for nobles like the Vorontsovs for their choice to stay in the countryside—to continue breeding pure borzoi, despite the hardships and lack of labor," Papa said. "Neither of us would be here today had they chosen to abandon country life for an easier, city way of living."

I glanced down at Zola. Everything about her was pure borzoi: long, lean, and elegant. I tried to imagine her as a sled dog or herding dog, and couldn't. Probably because I couldn't imagine where I'd be if the borzoi didn't exist.

After hours of pacing, when the clock struck midnight, Zola returned to the birthing nest. She tried to lie down, but couldn't quite get comfortable and sprang up again, circling round and round in the same spot, straining in an effort to force out a pup.

"Keep pushing," I encouraged Zola.

The first pup came quickly. Zola licked the sac off of the pup and with her teeth bit into the umbilical cord. She nudged the puppy to a nipple and the pup began to suckle.

Unlike the agony on Mama's face when she birthed Bohdan, Zola made it look easy.

An hour later the second pup was born. Zola went through the same routine without complication. Like clockwork the pups continued to come on the hour. They entered their new world smoothly and gave Papa and me little reason to worry.

Before dawn broke, Zola had birthed six pups: two brindles, one cream, a red, and two goldens. Papa kept checking Zola's nipples, as did I, throughout the night to ensure a nipple functioned for each pup. He also felt along the full length of Zola's abdomen to make sure that there were no more pups hiding inside.

"Our work is done," Papa said.

I checked on Zola a third time just to be certain,

worried that there might be a seventh pup—the one I had seen in my vision. Golden Rule Number Four: Trust, but verify.

"I feel a little lump," I said.

"Impossible, Lara. I just checked."

"I definitely feel something. Right here on her lower left side."

"Let me see." Papa's hands moved up and down her abdomen.

"There must be a seventh pup still inside."

"Hmmm . . . you may be right," Papa said, giving me a good pat on the back. *"Molodietz."*

"Do you think it's dead?" I wondered if this was why the white pup had faded in and out of my vision.

"Could be," Papa answered. "We need to get Zola moving again."

"To induce the pup," I finished for Papa. Quickly I grabbed a lead, but Zola resisted and wouldn't leave her pups. As Zar nudged her, slowly she began to walk with me in circles around the stall. I put her on a tight leash, for she kept pulling me toward her litter. Eventually green discharge dripped from her buttocks and I let her return to her litter.

Zola circled around and around, straining in an effort to push out the last pup.

"Good girl, Zola," I said. "Keep pushing."

Soon Zola was licking a pup, as white as snow, coaxing it to breathe for the first time.

"Look, *Tyatya*, a white pup. She looks just like Zar!"

Even before I could check her underside, I knew the pup was a girl. The Count would welcome her because of her pure white fur, a coat fit for royalty.

"How do you know the pup's a girl?" Papa asked.

"For the same reason I knew the pups would come tonight." I wanted to gloat, but something didn't seem right.

Why was Zola licking so hard?

She continued to lick harder, stroking the newborn with her tongue and nudging her to breathe. Zar whimpered and crept closer toward the pup.

"Easy, girl." Zola would hurt the pup if she didn't let up.

But she wouldn't stop, and the pup's pearly white coat slowly turned a dirty blue-gray color.

Papa bent down and put two fingers just underneath the newborn's belly. "Stoke the stove!"

I added more kindling to the fire while Papa took the pup and held her against his chest to warm her. With his free hand he massaged one of Zola's nipples until a milky liquid covered his fingertips. He tried to encourage the newborn to latch on to the nipple, but she just lay limp in Papa's big hands, unable to muster a shred of strength.

And just like the pup, Zola gave up, too, collapsing on top of the bear hide with the rest of her litter.

"We've got to save this pup!" I cried.

This didn't come to me in a vision. I could feel it in my gut. Something big depended on her. Something bigger than all of us.

I threw open the door to the cold cellar, where we stored perishables in a big hole dug in the ground of the stable floor. I grabbed two eggs, some goat milk, and mixed them together.

At least Papa didn't give up on her like he had on Zar.

With the bottle in hand I hurried into the birthing stall. I kissed the icon hanging above Zola one more time and sat down just underneath it, while the words from the prayer, "Hail Mary," raced through my head.

Papa placed the newborn on my chest. "Don't get your hopes up. She'd be easier to cull."

"Nothing's wasted in trying and we've got everything to gain, if she makes it." I took the nipple and dabbed drops of formula onto her lips, trying to get her to take the bottle. Please, I willed her. Drink.

She was so small and helpless against my chest. Her body felt like a lump of cold dough. I dabbed a few more drops onto her lips, and they just dribbled down her chest. Gently, I wiped her dry with one of the cotton towels.

Again I moved the nipple of the bottle along her mouth. Her head moved a tad, what looked like rooting, so I squeezed a few more drops between her lips. "Come on, girl."

Zar nudged the newborn gently on the rump, like any good parent urging his child to eat.

"Was that a wiggle?" I asked Zar with hope in my voice.

Zar nudged her again and licked her small face with his long red tongue.

Slowly, she started to root, her head bobbing up and down, and side to side.

"Here it is, girl." I put the nipple in front of her mouth. "Come on now, open up!"

The pup latched on and started to suckle. It gave me hope that she might make it. In my head, I named her Chara for the magical charm I knew she would one day work over all of us. I stroked her back with one finger ever so gently. "She took it, *Tyatya!*"

Papa grinned from ear to ear. "You're a splendid nurse, Lara."

His words fed my heart, for Papa seldom dished out compliments. When Chara finished suckling, I brought her over to Zola, holding her, cupped in both hands to let Zola sniff her. But Zola lifted her nose high in the air and rejected her.

Papa shrugged his shoulders. "Golden Rule Number Five: Mothers know best. I doubt this pup will make it."

He offered these words as if they would console me. Instead, they felt like lots of little needles, stabbing at my heart. To my mind, a good mama doesn't give up. She fights for *all* of her children, just like my mama.

Unlike Chara, each of the other pups nursed and looked as plump as a downy pillow.

"You've earned some sleep," Papa said to me, patting me on the shoulder.

A mighty smile came to my face. "I've earned more than sleep."

Papa tilted his head to one side. But it was the blank look on his face that scared me more. It was as empty as the nursing bottle I held in my hand. "Oh, the naming of the pups," he said.

"*Nyet*, the secret behind Golden Rule Number Eight," I said. "Remember?"

"Patience, *dorogaya*. I need to find the right words." Papa put his arms around me and kissed the top of my head.

I could wait for the secret behind Golden Rule Number Eight, if it bought me more time with the dogs. "Then it's only fair that while I wait, you let me see the last pup through her feedings until she's strong enough."

Papa harrumphed. "Then I must quickly find the words to reveal the secret to get you back under your mama's wings."

The little hope I had started to shrivel up. I felt empty, as if Papa could only see half of me, the part he wanted to see, the part that reminded him of Mama—the dark hair, the braids, and the amber eyes. He didn't see the stuff that mattered, the part that was just like him. The part that lived deep inside both of us, that drove us, that linked us to the dogs.

"Go home. Get some rest. You must be tired," Papa said. "You can name the pups later."

I wasn't about to budge.

Papa's brow bunched up. "Your little pup's in God's hands now."

"She needs both of us," I told him.

Just as Papa opened his mouth to say something, wolves started to howl. They sounded as if they were just outside the window. Zar pricked his ears, and he let out a loud bark. Zola nudged her pups in closer as Zar stormed around the stall in circles, barking nonstop, causing such a fuss he roused the borzoi in the other part of the stable to join the barking chorus.

And with all the commotion, the wolves we housed for training purposes began to howl, too.

Papa peered through the icy glass. "Wolves, just under the birches."

I rushed to the window with Chara in my hands. With the night sky on the brink of dawn, I could make out the silhouettes of three of them.

"That's him, *Tyatya*! The Red Thief has come back."

CHAPTER TEN

The Red Thief Returns

Two of the wolves howled, hiked on their haunches and noses pointed to the pinky-plum blue sky. Such powerful songs came from deep within their bellies.

The thought of them so close, standing under the birches Zar and I had passed—alone—in the dark of night frightened me. I cradled Chara even closer to me. "I thought wolves were afraid of us."

"Normally they are," Papa replied, pulling on his coat.

"Then why are they coming so close?"

But I answered my own question.

They must be desperate to eat.

"Don't worry." Papa headed for the rifle cabinet. "They'll learn soon enough that they aren't welcome here."

On cue, Zar flew over the birthing stall fence and

headed for the door to join Papa—his nose poking the latch and his feet dancing.

"*Nyet,* boy, stay," Papa said.

Zar pawed at the door, and the fur on his neck bristled.

"Let him hunt, *Tyatya.* He wants to go with you."

Papa grabbed a lead and dragged Zar, his feet flying like mad, his claws scarring up the dirt floor, to a spot where he tied him to one of the brass rings attached to the wall.

How Zar struggled to free himself, pulling and twisting and leaping toward the door. His front feet pawed the air like a rabid dog.

"Don't let him out," Papa said to me. "He'll get in the way."

"Zar has experience with the Red Thief."

"Zar's got experience, all right," Papa said. "Lucky for him Borei came when he did."

"Who told you?"

Papa kissed the hunting horn that hung around his neck three times, and then he disappeared. The kennel door slammed shut, followed by the music of his horn and a quick . . .

Boom!

The noise from the gun shook my insides. I braced myself for the next one, and even though pups are born deaf, I covered Chara's little ears just the same.

Boom! rang the second shot.

I prepared myself for a third one and closed my eyes, my whole body cringing.

Just like Papa had promised, the howling stopped. Little by little, the borzoi settled down.

Except for Zar. His ears still stood on alert, his focus unbreakable.

Papa returned, kicking the snow off his felt boots. He wore a look of defeat on his face. "They got away."

"*Tyatya,* you've got to train Zar," I said. "Look at how much he wants to hunt."

I expected Papa to walk away from me, as if he were deaf to my question. "Did you see how big the Red Thief was? He'd tear Zar to shreds."

Part of me wanted to stick up for Zar, and another part of me was afraid to lose him.

What if Papa was right?

Not long after Papa left to send a telegram to the Count with good news about the birth of the pups, the *zvon* of stable bells pulsed—*ding ding dong, ding ding dong, ding ding dong.* And even as the bells continued to ring like a chorus of singing icons, Alexander rushed in, wiping his tired, sleepy eyes.

"Did the pups come early?" The tone of his voice sounded worried.

"Everyone's fine," I assured him.

"You're always right where you're needed most, Larochka. You're like a crystal ball."

I needed to be more careful. How long could I keep my visions a secret from him?

Alexander felt Zola's abdomen first to make sure that there were no more pups hidden inside, just as Papa and I had done, and then Alexander inspected each of the six pups nestled close to Zola.

"They all look healthy." He patted Zar and Zola on the head.

"Except this one." I lifted her from my lap. "Her name's Chara."

Alexander's eyes widened. "I don't dare ask how you came up with that name, nor do I doubt she'll work her charm over all of us." Alexander knelt down beside me. Gently, he took her from my hands and cradled her against his neck. "What happened?"

"Zola rejected her," I answered.

Alexander kissed her on the rump before handing her back to me. "Then she'd better work her charm over Zola soon."

"She'll need help over the first few weeks." I laid Chara across my chest, and ran my finger along her spine. "She shows promise."

Alexander ran his finger along her spine, too, and nodded. "She does!"

"Did you see the wolves?" I asked Alexander.

Zar's ears shot up, and he bounded over to the window.

"Unfortunately not." Alexander joined Zar and peered through the veil of lacy frost that covered the glass panes. He stood there and wiped away the frost with his bare hands, creating visible gaps here and there, as he looked out. "I heard the Red Thief weaseled his way into the stable and got to our livestock again."

Even in his frustration, Alexander's voice was kind and gentle.

"When the wind dies down, we'll get the Red Thief." Alexander said it more to Zar than to me, and then glided his hand along the arch of his back. "Right, boy?"

Zar responded with a little dance. And my heart danced, too.

"Have you talked to my papa about training Zar?"

"Don't worry, Larochka. I know how important this is to you," he answered. "I will."

I glanced up at the icon of the mother staring down at her child with such love in her eyes. She reminded me of my own mama. And she also reminded me of the kind of love I had for Zar. "I don't know how I'd fill my days without the dogs."

"Me too," Alexander said. "Father begs me to join him and take over the bell foundry with my older brother, promising me there is no other work more fulfilling than making bells for the Tsar's churches."

I hoped that day wouldn't come too soon. With Alexander gone, the Woronzova Kennel would be like a crown without the jewels. "Would you have to live in Moscow like your brother?"

"For now, no—Father's agreed to give me a chance to live my dream and make something of this kennel. I have two years. If I don't produce borzoi worthy of the Tsar, I agreed to join him."

"You'll succeed," I told him. "I'll do whatever I can to help you."

"You should get some sleep," Alexander said. "Your eyes look tired."

"Chara needs me—"

"I'll see to her myself," Alexander said. "I give you my word."

A promise from a noble meant something. Keeping one was a higher honor than dying for the Tsar, Golden Rule Number One—and my personal favorite because this Rule gave everyone willing to live by his word a chance to be noble, whether born into nobility or not.

Alexander took Chara from my hands and cuddled her against his chest. "Take Zar for protection."

"Do you think the wolves will be back?"

"They wouldn't dare with Zar by your side," he said. "For certain the Red Thief would remember him."

On my way home, I stopped at the chapel to light a candle for Chara. Part of me hoped I might find Ruslan. While Pushkin's words touched my soul and gave me strength, Ruslan's words made me think.

I approached the icon of the Virgin Mary, bent down on both knees, and genuflected. I walked over to the candles and pulled out a long, slender taper from the glass jar. I placed it over a burning flame until it caught fire, and then lit a candle for Chara. As I thought of her pudgy little face, I lit another candle . . . and another . . . and another . . . until all of the candles had been lit and glowed brightly.

"You're going to burn the place down with so many candles," Ruslan said when he entered the chapel.

I told him about the Red Thief returning, about Zola and the birth, as well as about the bet I had with Papa, and how we almost lost Chara. "This pup has to live. I don't know why just yet. Even Papa helped."

"Maybe your father's coming around?"

"Maybe." I sensed that Papa was struggling with something.

"Change is what we all fear at some level. Once we learn to embrace it, only then can it become our friend. It's the first step, but a difficult one."

I wondered if the first step to change was part of a bigger plan. And did God play a part in that plan. "Does God speak to you through your work?"

Ruslan chuckled. "That's an odd question."

"It would seem so to me." Nobody could paint figures like Ruslan did, figures that looked so saintly they could float off the wood they were painted on and join us for tea, unless God had a say in it.

Ruslan looked around as if he worried someone might overhear him, and instead of speaking his answer, he nodded his head, and then he whispered, "I like to think that God has a hand in my work."

"My mama believes in such things, too," I whispered back to him.

"What about you?" he asked.

When I thought of Papa and his Rules, the very ones my ancestors had passed down for generations, I knew I fought to fit in and be just like Papa and all the other kennel stewards before him. But every time I had a vision, I saw nothing evil in using it to guide me to do the right thing. And every time I kept quiet, I felt like I was betraying my gift. My eyes dropped to the floor. "I don't know what to think."

"In these times, a gift from God can be dangerous," Ruslan said. "One shouldn't fight it. One should use the gift for good."

"My mama says the same thing." Still, I was afraid.

I didn't want to risk losing everything that mattered to me.

Alexander.

My family.

Zola and the dogs, and especially Zar.

CHAPTER ELEVEN

Red Snow

I slept soundly and woke the next morning to thrashing pain along my forehead, dreading the evil that I knew would come. I keeled over, gripping my forehead, to alleviate the crushing pain. I tried to force my eyes to stay open so I wouldn't see what was coming, but the pain was too much. When I closed my eyes, I saw Zar's littermates Borei, Sila, and Bistri—chasing the Red Thief, trying to separate it from its pack.

The image brought me joy.

I squeezed my eyes more tightly. I had to see more. I had to know the outcome.

As soon as the vision faded, another appeared—one of red-drenched snow, and lots of it.

And then that image faded, too.

Was it blood?

But whose?

Surely, it belonged to the wolves.

In my gut I wasn't convinced. I had to find a way to stop this hunt from happening.

When I opened my eyes, I found Mama looking down at me, her lacy, woolen shawl wrapped around her tiny shoulders. In her arms lay Bohdan, nursing.

"Another vision?" Mama asked.

I sat up from my sleeping bench. A cold ball of fear settled in my stomach. "Something awful's about to happen. I must warn Papa."

"He's at the kennel," Mama said. "Don't be afraid. There's a reason God is speaking to you."

"*Matushka,* if Papa believes in God, why is he against my visions?"

"That is for him to tell you," Mama said. "When he does, you'll understand."

Balled up on a pallet of straw in a cocoon by our front door, Zar stood up, stretched and arched his back, and then shook the snow off his coat. Together we headed to the kennel first to check on Chara in the birthing room. When we reached it, I found Alexander, cuddled up just underneath the Mother with Child icon.

I expected Chara to be in Alexander's arms, but she wasn't. "Did she—" I couldn't bring myself to say it.

"No, she didn't die. Chara's fine." Alexander pointed to Zola and my eyes followed.

There, among the other pups nestled between Zola's long legs, lay a pudgy ball of white, nursing. She looked so much like her father, Zar, when he was a pup.

"That's amazing! How did you get Zola to accept her so quickly?"

He shrugged his shoulders. "It was Chara's charm that did it."

"You're too humble," I said. It was his patience that had won out with Zola. I stroked Chara's back with one finger and she responded with a bob of her head.

"She's through the tough part, Larochka," Alexander said. "Thanks for being there when Zola needed you."

Alexander made me feel like I belonged exactly where I was, and that I had earned it on my own—and not through a birthright.

"My father wants to go after the Red Thief," Alexander said.

"When?"

"Today," he answered.

All I could see was red snow. "Which dogs are you taking?"

"The usual team—Borei, Bistri, and Sila," Alexander answered. "Plus Zar."

Zar's ears perked. He jumped up on Alexander and rested his paws on Alexander's shoulders. A pang of jealousy hit me.

"Did Papa agree to take him?" Four dogs went against Golden Rule Number Six. Anyone who hunted, especially Alexander, knew that three borzoi make up a team.

"Not yet," Alexander said. "I know what you're thinking, but it's time the Rules become more flexible."

I wanted to warn him, to tell him to postpone the hunt. But Alexander would want to know why, and I couldn't tell him. *A promise is a promise.*

"Do you know where I can find my papa?"

"He's in the tack room," Alexander answered.

"Sorry to rush away, Sasha. I've got to take care of something." And then I took off in a sprint.

"What's happened?" Alexander called out to me.

I pretended not to hear him.

When I entered the tack room, Papa already had his hunting horn around his neck. He spoke before I could even say a word. "You can't come."

"That's not what I'm here about."

"That's good to hear." Papa quickly busied himself with a cowhide lead that needed mending.

"We're taking our best team of dogs and we'll get the Red Thief, once and for all," Papa said.

He struggled to fix the lead. His fingers fumbled with it, and I could see that all of this weighed on him.

"Let me," I offered, taking the broken lead from his clumsy hands. I rewove the three strands of leather as tightly as I could to create one strong, single lead. Then I bound the strands together with six silver clips that Papa positioned along the lead in equal intervals. I shined the silver with the cuff of my shirt, admiring the decorative clip stamped with the Vorontsov coat of arms: a double-headed Tsarist eagle perched above two gray-white Orlov Trotters. The inscribed motto, *Semper Immota Fides*, captured the Vorontsov family value of steadfast loyalty.

"Easy now," Papa said.

I lifted the hammer above one of the clips. Ever so gently, I tapped down on each of them with the head of the hammer to lock the braid in place.

When I finished, I handed the lead back to Papa, who inspected it from top to bottom with a careful eye. "It's impeccable," he said with more than a hint of pride in his voice.

Papa gestured in a way that reminded me of the old Papa—the one who let me shadow him around the kennel. "I know how much you love the dogs." For a brief second he paused, as if he reconsidered his thoughts. But the new Papa—the one with a son—spoke instead. "But you'll be better off with a husband. The midwife tells me she has a nephew."

Before I could say a word, Papa's eyes narrowed on

Alexander approaching us from the stalls. Prancing alongside him were Borei, Bistri, Sila, and Zar.

When Zar saw me, he bounded straight ahead of the others. He nudged my hand and licked it. I stroked his silky coat of white fur and scratched behind his tiny, tucked-back ears. The others joined him and wiggled their way next to me, goosing me with their long noses for my attention.

Alexander popped into the tack room. "I need a longer lead." He searched the walls for one among those hanging. He chose the white one I had just mended to match his long white gloves and the coats of the dogs, as was custom.

Although I tried to hide it, I grinned from ear to ear.

"What's *he* doing here?" Papa grunted, pointing at Zar.

"I'd like to try something new," Alexander said.

"Three's the lucky number," Papa reminded him.

"How will Zar ever learn to properly kill a wolf, if he never trains with a team?" Alexander asked.

"An inexperienced borzoi is a dead one," Papa said. "Golden Rule Number Seven." He crossed his arms and stood rooted to the ground.

"He has experience with the Red Thief," Alexander shot back.

"And nearly got himself killed," Papa said.

"Zar held his own, despite no proper training. He's got a keen instinct I've never seen in a borzoi."

"It's not the way we do things." Papa expected everyone to follow the Golden Rules like a row of ducklings tottering faithfully behind their mother.

"I respect your Rules. Still, we need to strive to improve our hunting methods, even if it means breaking the Rules," Alexander said. "Of course, my father could settle this when he gets here. But it's your cooperation I'd like to gain."

Papa threw up his hands, shaking his head. He bent down and stroked Borei. "If anyone outsmarts the Red Thief, it'll be Borei. If you insist on bringing Zar, so be it, but he stays on the sledge. I don't want him getting in the way of the hunt."

Alexander extended his hand to Papa. "That's a fair compromise," he said, and before he hurried off with all four dogs tethered to the lead I had just mended, he gave me a warm wink.

Once Alexander was out of earshot, words of warning lined up on my tongue and took aim. But they got lodged in my throat.

You can do it, I told myself.

Mama's voice stepped in, too. *Trust, Lara, trust.*

As did Ruslan's. *Don't fight it.*

Just as I rallied enough courage to speak up, Count Vorontsov entered the stable in heavy furs that draped to the floor.

"We must hurry and finish preparing for the hunt," Papa snarled. "Load the sledge."

"I need to talk to you," I said to Papa. "It's important."

He did an about-face and walked off to greet the Count.

In the manner fitting a good soldier, and against my judgment, and like I've done before every hunt since I could remember, I found the medicine box, checked the contents, added more towels, and loaded it on the long, open sledge. In the storage closet I rifled through the blankets and tossed some into the back section of the sledge. Although I rarely packed guns, I did so this time just in case. I feared they would need them.

As Papa lined up glasses of vodka for himself, the Count, and Alexander, I crept to an open corner of the sledge where the hunters stacked the dead wolves to carry back upon their return. I had never defied Papa before, but he left me no choice.

I had to go on the hunt.

To stop whatever bad was coming.

"To Borei's success," Papa said with a raised glass.

They clinked glasses, downed the vodka in one gulp, and picked up another glass.

"To the health of the dogs," Alexander toasted. Again they clinked glasses and downed the vodka like water.

They picked up their last glass of vodka.

"To catching the Red Thief," the Count toasted.

Just as Papa threw his head back to down the vodka, I tucked myself into a tiny ball in the corner of the sledge and ducked underneath a couple of blankets. I didn't dare move and prayed Papa wouldn't find me.

"Where's Lara? She was supposed to load the sledge," Papa said. From the jingle of his keys, I could hear him come toward the sledge, and then the medicine box hinge creaked open.

"What's this?" Anger coursed through Papa's voice.

My heart hammered. I was certain he would grab me by the cuff of my coat and haul me off the sledge.

"We don't need so many towels," Papa grumbled.

I opened my eyes and exhaled.

The *clip-clop* of hooves came closer. "Steady, now," Boris said to the horses. With the forward and backward lurching of the sledge, the horses snorted, until they finally settled into the leather tackle that crisscrossed their bodies.

Alexander then whistled three quick notes and one by one I felt the team of borzoi spring up onto the back of the sledge. I imagined them leaping as ballerinas do and wondered how a breed of such nobility and elegance ever managed to hunt wolves. Their lean, willowy bodies seemed more suited for the ballroom than in a snowy field chasing wolves.

"Lie down," Alexander directed the dogs.

The back of the sledge wasn't spacious. So I felt a few of them circle around, before curling into a comfortable position. It would only be a matter of time before they would sense my presence.

Alexander covered the dogs and the heaviness of the hide's fringe fell around me, building a wall, like a cozy nest. "We're ready," he called up to Papa.

"As am I," said the Count from his horse, who was chafing at the bit.

Then came the long blow of Papa's horn—a sound I longed to make—followed by the *zvon* of stable bells to send us off with luck. The horn and bells set off a chorus of dogs—barking and yelping and howling—eager to join us. For they knew where we were headed and that they were being left behind.

"Onward!" Papa shouted.

He cracked his knout and the sledge moved forward through the crunch of packed snow and ice. The cold air cut through the blankets and hides and chilled my bones. As much as I wanted to curl up with the borzoi for extra warmth, I stayed put in my own nest of blankets.

Alexander recited legends of past hunts in a way I imagined he'd share fairy tales with his children at bedtime. His stories about the first borzoi on the estate and the clever tactics they used when hunting wolves kept the dogs quiet, while Papa steered the sledge behind the Count on horseback in pursuit of the wolves.

In the distance, I could hear a chorus of wolves howling, warning each other almost, as if they knew we were coming and why. Pushkin's poem about a winter journey came to mind.

> *Down the dismal snow-track swinging*
> *Speeds the troika, and the drone*

The next words came to me differently from what I had learned, and they were laced with dread.

> *Of the wolf-pack's frightful howling*
> *Numbs me with its hungry tone.*

We would chase the howls and follow the pack for as long as it took until we were close enough to the wolves. Only then would the command be given to release the team of borzoi.

One of the dogs started to fidget, and then I heard Zar's playful whimper, his paws digging at my blanket. I fought to keep hold of the blanket that covered me.

"Settle down," Alexander demanded.

"Is everything all right?" Papa called from up front.

"Something's gotten into Zar," Alexander answered.

"We never should have brought him," Papa shouted. "He's already a nuisance."

"It's too late to change our minds now," the Count said.

Afraid Alexander might reach and grab for the hides that must have fallen off of Zar, I turtled my knees even tighter into my chest until they jabbed against my chin. Still, the sledge offered only so much room and in Alexander's effort to cover Zar he tripped over my foot and landed on top of me.

"*Oi,*" I whimpered.

When he pulled the hide off of me, I could see the surprised look on his face, and quickly brought my finger up to my lips. "Shhh."

"Larochka!" The look on Alexander's face told me not to worry.

"You won't tell, Sasha?" I whispered.

Alexander shook his head. "Did you bring your hunting knife?"

I nodded and pointed to my pocket.

He leaned in and whispered into my ear, "Good, you might need it."

I didn't feel good about what was coming.

I was drowning in worry.

CHAPTER TWELVE

The Hunt

Eventually the sledge came to a stop. "Wolves, up ahead, two of them," the Count called from his horse. "Get the dogs into position."

"One of them looks like the Red Thief," Papa added. And then came the blast of the horn to signal to the dogs that wolves had been sighted.

Alexander pantomimed for me to stay down and covered my head with a blanket. I hardly risked Papa's wrath to stay completely hidden. I poked my head back out from underneath the blanket and prayed Papa would one day forgive me for disobeying.

Lined up at the edge of the sledge stood Bistri, followed by Sila, and then Borei. How I wished it were me holding their lead. Sila was first to see the wolves in the distance and gave a little yelp. Her feet danced with such excitement, the others danced, too.

"*Ou-la-lou! Ta-ra! Ta-ra!*" With those words Alexander slipped the lead and one by one, the dogs plunged into the untouched, powdery snow from the sledge. As they coursed and cut through the snow, with Borei in the lead—running as fast as the north wind—bits of snow sprayed from underneath their feet into the air. If it weren't for their black noses and the champagne-colored patches along their rumps and backs, I would have lost them from sight against the snow.

Papa clucked his tongue to get the horses moving again to follow the dogs.

Poor Zar. How he cried to be part of the team!

It was how I felt, too, watching him struggle to free himself to join his littermates. Alexander brought him up to the front of the sledge and tied Zar's lead to a hook in a triple sailor knot. It took all of Alexander's strength to restrain Zar, he pulled so hard.

Within seconds, the dogs thrust themselves in the midst of the two wolves, trying to separate the Red Thief from its new mate.

Now there were four wolves!

And the pack seemed to be growing—trickling out from the woods with bristled manes, growling, and baring fangs.

Was this normal? I wanted to ask Alexander, for something felt very wrong.

Papa whipped the horses and they picked up speed.

"The dogs need Zar," Alexander called out.

"Zar will only get in the way," Papa answered.

"Father, our team is outnumbered," Alexander persisted.

"Borei can handle it, son," the Count said.

Papa pulled the horses to a halt. They bucked and reared and neighed in fright, but Papa regained control with a jerk of the reins.

The wolves circled the borzoi. From opposite ends the wolves took turns lunging at them. Waves of snow flew into the air as the borzoi leaped and squirmed to avoid the attacks.

Borei tried to lead a way out for Sila and Bistri. Every time he found an opening, the gap closed.

There was nowhere to turn. The circle had tightened and closed in on them.

Suddenly the Red Thief charged the dogs, followed by a mass of wolfy gray and silver from all angles. Two of the borzoi emerged from the attack, hurdling over the tangle of wolves, as if they had wings that carried them.

The third borzoi lay in the snow. I recognized his piercing cry—*nyet!*

Not Borei—not Papa's favorite dog!

The Red Thief had Borei by the throat, while the other wolves gnawed and attacked at his legs.

Sila and Bistri tried to help Borei. Each time they made an advance to rescue him, they were received with curled lips, snapped at, and pushed back.

There were too many wolves.

Do something! I wanted to scream at Papa. I couldn't bear to watch. At the same time, my eyes wouldn't close.

Papa pulled out his rifle. He shot it into the air.

Boom!

Some of the wolves scattered.

The Count fired a second shot into the air.

Boom!

Fewer wolves dashed away.

Zar pulled and yanked with such force, I thought he'd break his neck or open up his wounds if he didn't free himself.

As the Count reloaded his rifle, Papa bolted out of the sledge and hastened toward the chaos of wolves and dogs. I had never seen him barrel through the snow in such panic. He cursed at the wolves, words I had never heard him use before.

"I'll take the left side," the Count called out.

"Stay here and get your knife ready," Alexander whispered to me. He grabbed a rifle and followed Papa and the Count.

I pulled my knife out and got myself ready. Ready for what, I wasn't sure. All I knew was that I wanted to help, too. If only I had packed a fourth rifle and knew how to use it!

The Count took a shot.

Boom!

The first wolf fell.

Papa reloaded his rifle and shot at the wolves on the perimeter of the tangle.

Boom!

One of the wolves yelped and sank into the snow. Others ran away. As Papa reloaded the chamber of his rifle, Alexander fired.

Boom!

Another wolf crumpled into the snowy whiteness.

Like the devil it was, the Red Thief didn't frighten as easily as before. It stood over Borei, scarfing mouthfuls of the blood-soaked snow around it and swallowing with shameful pleasure.

Surely they needed Zar. But I kept hearing Papa's voice: *Three is the lucky number, not four.*

All three hunters aimed their rifles at the Red Thief standing over Borei. They had a clean shot.

"Take it," Papa said to the Count.

"My son deserves it," the Count said.

Somebody shoot! my heart screamed.

Nobody dared, for Sila and Bistri suddenly rejoined the mix and lunged at the Red Thief.

Papa raised his hunting horn to his lips and blew the command for the dogs to retreat. Sila and Bistri ignored the signal.

"Off!" the Count ordered.

"Off!" Alexander echoed.

The dogs ignored their commands, too!

Borei no longer cried. Nor did he struggle to get free. He just lay there.

I had to do something!

"Sila, Bistri, off!" I called in desperation.

Bistri retreated first, followed by Sila. Papa glanced back at the sledge.

"*Tyatya,* watch out!" I shrieked.

The Red Thief had stepped over Borei and slowly advanced on Papa in a crouched position, ready to spring.

Papa aimed his rifle at it and took a shot.

Boom!

The wolf buckled in its back leg. Still, the big silvery-red-tipped beast continued toward Papa, limping on three legs. As Papa reloaded, the Count took another shot.

Boom!

The shot grazed the wolf and it stumbled, but it recovered its footing. Alexander lifted his rifle, steadied it, and took a shot.

Boom!

Alexander's shot missed.

With eyes locked on Papa, the wolf suddenly rushed for him.

"Look out, *Tyatya!*" I warned, wringing my hands.

Papa took aim and pulled the trigger. I heard it click, but nothing came out. He pulled again and again without results, and quickly shifted the rifle into his hands, swinging it, as if it were a sword, trying to keep the wolf back.

The wolf circled Papa.

It was so close to Papa, neither the Count nor Alexander could get a clean shot.

Trust my gift, I kept telling myself.

It rang through my mind like a pealing bell in a blinding blizzard leading me home.

When I couldn't bear to watch another second, I untied Zar's lead and freed him. "Get him, Zar! The Red Thief is yours!"

Zar tore off the sledge into the snow for the Red Thief—hitting it hard, knocking it to the ground. Taking Zar's lead, Bistri and Sila followed and worked to distract the wolf, nipping at its back legs. Zar and the Red Thief struggled for each other's throats. I expected the bullet in the wolf's back leg to slow it down. It only made the wolf angrier. And although the wolf was bigger, Zar was quicker and maneuvered around its lunges until Zar attacked with swift and powerful pluck.

Zar got hold of the wolf's throat and threw it to the ground with such force, I heard a snap and prayed for a broken neck. While Zar pinned the Red Thief by its neck, Bistri and Sila each caught hold of a hind leg.

"*Molodietz*, Zar!" I yelled.

Papa kept staring at Zar. His face was not filled with anger, like I had expected it might be, but of fear—as if a ghost from his past haunted him.

Alexander rushed to the dogs and thrust his knife into the Red Thief's heart, stepped aside, and called the dogs off. Bistri and Sila released the wolf and limped to Alexander's side. Zar stood over the Red Thief, his chest puffed out with pride. Pools of courage filled his dark, almond-shaped eyes.

My first vision.

It had finally come true.

Happy and relieved as I was, I couldn't speak and I just stood there, taking it all in.

Papa rushed to Borei, collapsing to his knees beside him. He placed his ear next to Borei's heart.

"He's dead," Papa said through muffled cries, holding his stomach like someone had punched him.

I had never heard Papa cry before.

Papa gently picked Borei up and carried him across

the field dotted with dead wolves. Sila and Bistri trailed behind him like nervous shadows, sniffing at Borei's dangling feet. Splotches of red against the champagne-white dappled their silky coats. Zar joined them, his head carried low.

Alexander shook his head with grief. "I'm so sorry." Then he joined his father, the Count, to collect the dead wolves.

The wolves that had gotten away resumed howling. Their cries of grief gushed upward in powerful, heart-wrenching rushes—and mirrored what stirred inside of me.

I turned to gather the leads to secure Sila, Bistri, and Zar—and a gray wolf jumped onto the sledge, baring its fangs at me, coiled up in a hunched position, ready to spring. The troika of horses yoked together started to nervously buck up and kick.

Gospodi! I took a step backward and nearly stumbled.

Be brave, I thought. Wolves prey on fear.

I gripped Alexander's knife more tightly and thrust it at the wolf, hoping to scare it off.

It didn't scare.

"Lara, stay calm. I'm coming to help," Papa called, cradling Borei close to his chest.

"Me too!" Alexander yelled.

Boom!

Boom!

Their shots into the sky didn't spook the gray wolf. Instead, they angered it.

Just then, Zar jumped up onto the sledge and surprised the wolf. The two of them snapped at each other—back and forth—until Zar plucked it by its throat and flipped it hard on its back.

A loud crack followed.

A broken neck.

A dead wolf.

I collapsed to my knees in relief, as Papa, Alexander, and the Count rushed to the sides of the sledge with their rifles aimed at the gray wolf.

"*Molodietz*, Zar," Alexander said. "You got him."

"I'll hold my aim just in case," Papa said to Alexander. "This one's yours."

"Take it, son," the Count said.

"Lara deserves the honor," Alexander said.

"She isn't capable," Papa barked.

"*Tyatya*, you're wrong." I stood up with my knife held out in front of me. Certainly I could slit the heart of a dead wolf.

"What's Lara doing with *your* knife?" Papa asked Alexander.

"You can do it," Alexander said.

I mustered all the courage I had.

"Good dog, Zar. Now, off!" I was afraid I'd accidentally stab him.

Zar didn't obey. He held on to the gray wolf.

"Off, Zar," I said again.

Again, Zar didn't obey.

And then the gray wolf attempted to wriggle free. Zar held his grip and didn't let go.

"You were right to disobey," I said to Zar.

"You'll need to pierce through the ribs to get to the heart," Alexander coached.

Cautiously, I approached the wolf.

"We're losing time," Papa said.

It wasn't until Papa started to climb up onto the sledge that I was moved to action. I swallowed a lump of fear the size of an iceberg and thrust the knife into the wolf's heart.

Blood spurted.

Onto me.

Onto Zar.

Everywhere.

"You did it," Alexander cheered.

"You were right about Zar," the Count teased Papa. "What a nuisance!"

I put my arms around my knight of knights. "*We* did it, Zar."

Papa leaned over the side of the sledge and patted Zar on the head. "You've done good tonight, boy. You've done good tonight, too," he said to me. "But you disobeyed me."

"I had good cause, *Tyatya*."

"The reason is unimportant." Little blue veins popped out on Papa's neck. "You don't belong out here, and there'll be consequences."

Papa's shoulders slumped. He retrieved Borei and lifted him from the snow stained in blood and placed him on a blanket in the back of the sledge.

Papa brought his hunting horn to his lips and kissed it three times, and then he blew into it—long and low to warn the kennel hands back at the stable that the hunt had gone bad. Papa climbed up onto the sledge, buried his face in Borei's fur, and lay there clutching him. Then Papa covered Borei in a blanket and made the sign of the cross. "You're in God's hands now."

The Count and Alexander dragged the dead wolves and lifted them up onto the sledge, stacking them one on top of the other. There were five of them.

Had it been worth it?

The Red Thief had so much blood on his mouth, Borei's blood. I couldn't bear to look.

If only I had found a way to save Borei.

It was my fault for not speaking up.

The guilt and hurt that I felt was raw and exposed, as if one of my legs had just been chewed off.

I covered the rest of the wolves with blankets to purge them from my thoughts.

CHAPTER THIRTEEN

The Black Box

For several weeks after the hunt, Papa remained to himself. The only shimmer of joy I saw on his face was when he held Bohdan and that wasn't all that frequent, since Papa spent most of his time at the kennel. When our paths did cross, Papa barely acknowledged me and often darted away in a new direction, as if I were a skunk with a raised tail.

"Papa won't talk to me, *Matushka*. His silence is worse than his bark."

"Losing Borei has been hard on him, even more so when I told him that you had wanted to warn him not to go on the hunt," Mama said. "He has much to think about now. His whole world of beliefs and Rules has flip-flopped. He's struggling to sort it all out and make it right for you, himself, and the future of the dogs. Give him time to mull over all of this. I have faith that he'll come around and accept your visions for the gift that it is." Mama's smile hugged me. "I wish I could tell you more. The rest should come from your papa. When it does, it shall all make sense. Patience, *dorogaya*."

"I'm tired of being patient. I want things between me and Papa to return to what it once was—before Bohdan was born, when Papa let me shadow him at the kennel."

"Be careful what you wish for, Larochka."

At first, I shrugged away Mama's advice. There was nothing I cherished more than my childhood memories of Papa and the dogs. But her words lingered with me.

During Papa's period of silence, I split my time between my kennel chores at Mama's urging, as well as my responsibilities caring for Bohdan. I couldn't bear letting all the work fall on Mama. Despite coming from hardy stock, Mama had slowed since Bohdan's birth.

Not surprisingly, news about Zar had spread quickly. Requests to breed him with other borzoi from other kennels came in every day by telegram. Zar had become a regional hero. Yet Papa still refused to acknowledge Zar for the fearless hunter that he was.

Papa's gloomy mood over the loss of Borei seemed to have cast a spell over the entire kennel and its staff. Nothing lifted Papa's spirits—not even the Count's announcement of a celebration in joint honor of Zola's litter—as was tradition—and of Zar's triumph over the Red Thief. Around Papa his staff behaved in a mournful manner. As soon as Papa was out of earshot, all anyone, including Maxim, could chirp about was the upcoming celebration and the champagne and caviar upon which we would feast.

The night of the celebration, under a near-full moon, I took my favorite red ribbon from my braid and tied it around Zar's neck. Mama and I wore our best clothing made of red brocade with gold ribbon borders and donned matching headdresses decorated in gold galloons that Mama had made for special occasions. At Mama's insistence, Papa put on his finest shirt, and then he groomed the long black hairs of his beard. He ripped through the knots without a single flinch, as if all feeling had left him, as if life no longer existed inside him.

Mama took the brush from him and gently combed through the knots. "Smile, dear husband. There's much about which to be joyous."

"Of that I don't doubt, for the Count wouldn't extend his hospitality over nothing," Papa said. "But I'm lost inside myself. I can't find my way to the truth."

Until I had learned to trust my gift, I, too, had felt lost inside myself. Part of me wanted to fit in and follow in Papa's boots and live by the Golden Rules, as he and his forefathers had always done. Another part of me saw the good in my gift, for my visions spoke the truth to me and had become too real to ignore.

"Trust in yourself, *Tyatya*," I said. "You'll find the truth."

For the first time since the hunt, Papa's eyes met mine. He stared into them, as if the truth lived inside of me. "Do your visions come to you behind your eyelids?" he asked.

Papa caught me by surprise. "Yes, how did you guess?"

"I understand more than you think, Lara."

Thousands of twinkling lights glimmered from the ballroom's chandeliers and reflected off of the gilded moldings. Vast oils of past hunts and former Counts with their dogs hung from the ceiling to the waxed parquet floors. Best of all, Zar was received in a manner fitting his new status and Papa's staff chanted Zar's name in a play on words with the word *Tsar*.

"Long live Zar! Long live Zar! Long live Zar!" everyone chanted.

It even made Papa smile.

Soon the servants joined the chorus, as did the guests. The noise woke Bohdan and though startled at first, he, too, eventually blended into the singing buzz with his babbling. Zar held his head a little higher and puffed out his chest as he pranced beside me toward the tables that lined the perimeter. On them were set all of the usual foods to celebrate the birth of a litter: black caviar served on silver platters, sour cream brimming from crystal bowls, stacks of warm *blini* wrapped in linen spun from silk, and stuffed suckling pig dressed in horseradish.

In honor of Zar were two roasted pigs spread out along a grand table that could easily sit thirty people. They were the biggest pigs I'd ever seen.

Ornate mahogany stations were set up in each corner of the grand ballroom. Upon each station sat sparkling flutes arranged in tidy rows. Buckets upon buckets of iced champagne, primed and ready to be served, covered the outer perimeter of the floor.

"I should preside among my staff on the dais," Papa said. As if I were invisible, he bent down and kissed Bohdan's nose, and then he left Mama and me.

For as long as I could remember, I had always joined Papa and his team on the dais in celebratory moments like this one. I willed Papa to turn around and invite me, too, but he kept walking.

With Bohdan in one arm, Mama wrapped her free arm around me. "Where you stand tonight holds no relevance, Lara. What matters most is the truth."

"Still, it hurts. Zar belongs up there more than anyone," I said, stroking his head.

"Your papa's stubborn and will eventually come around," Mama said. "He loves his work too much not to. Which reminds me. If I hope to keep my job, I should check on the Countess. She's wearing a gown with a back zipper that's as stubborn as your papa. Will you be all right?"

I nodded and tried to take Bohdan from Mama.

"I'll keep him. This is just as much your night," she said.

Despite so much tasty food around me I wasn't hungry. Still, I heaped spoonfuls of suckling pig, Zar's favorite, onto a small plate and fed him one piece at a time, which he gently took from my fingers.

"Congratulations!" Ruslan rushed up and gave me a mighty pat on the back.

I almost didn't recognize him all cleaned up in a crisp, saintly white shirt.

"Everyone's talking about Zar," Ruslan said. "You must be proud of him."

"For me he's still the same splendid dog."

"Of course he is," Ruslan said. "Give others a chance to catch up to what you intimately know about Zar. Sometimes there are hurdles in front of us of which we're unaware."

"You're right." For something weighed on Papa. I could feel it.

"In memory of this big moment I've made something for you." Ruslan pulled a small black lacquer box of papier-mâché from his pocket and handed it to me.

On top was painted an almost iconic image of a white borzoi true to Zar from head to toe, standing proudly over a dead wolf of silvery-red-tipped color. I fingered Zar's face, as if it were really his, for Ruslan captured the pools of courage in his almond-shaped eyes. Around the edge of the box were swirls of gilded curls—a tiny detail that matched the curls of Zar's white frill.

"You made this—for me?"

"From all the stories I heard about the hunt from you, Alexander, and the Count, I couldn't get Zar's image out of my mind," Ruslan said. "So I painted him out of my head so I could proceed with my real work."

I placed the small black box in front of Zar. Like any dog hopeful for a bite of meat, Zar eagerly sniffed it and quickly lost interest.

"Hopefully, it pleases you more than it did Zar," Ruslan joked.

"It does. Thank you, Ruslan. I'll keep it for as long as I live."

"The box is small enough to fit in your pocket," Ruslan said. "No matter what, Zar will always be close to you."

Just then, a trumpet sounded and the Count and his family made their grand entrance into the ballroom. The Count and Alexander proudly wore their military uniforms in honor of the Tsar. The Countess drew *oohs* and *aahs* for the rich, deep blue silk gown she wore with diamonds sewn around its jeweled neck. In her arms she carried Almaz, wearing a diamond-encrusted collar in a pattern similar to the one around the neck of the Countess's dress.

The Count took a position on the dais next to Papa. He looked more tired than usual, and worn down. His bookkeeper stepped forward and handed Papa a bag of gold rubles. Papa nodded to the Count and tried to look pleased, but I could tell from Papa's eyes that no amount of gold rubles could replace Borei.

"May the festivities begin," the Count announced. In one hand the Count picked up his saber and in the other a bottle of champagne. He took the saber and grazed it along the side of the bottle several times until he beheaded the bottle in one quick slash. Champagne bubbled out as he handed the bottle to one of the servers. The Count continued to open dozens of bottles—one after another—in the same manner.

The servers quickly poured champagne into toasting flutes. They served the Count and his family first, and then came Papa, Maxim, and the rest of his kennel hands. Zar and I should have been among those standing around the table with Papa.

When everyone had a glass, the Count raised his high above his head. "To another healthy litter! May there be more white pups like Zar in the future!" As the Count took a sip, he added, "Long live Tsar Nicholas!" He nodded first to his wife, and then to Alexander and Papa, and then to each of the kennel staff until he finally nodded to the rest of us.

I clinked glasses with Ruslan, and then like everyone else in the room we followed the Count's lead and took a long sip.

Alexander spoke next. "To friendship!" He smiled at me and raised his glass.

Again Ruslan and I clinked glasses and drank along with everyone else in the room. Spirits were on the rise. I could feel it in the air.

Papa raised his glass and spoke third, nodding first to the Count, and then to Alexander. "To those of us who can't be here," he toasted in honor of Borei.

When Papa lowered his glass, the Count followed with a closing toast. "To Ryczar—the knight of knights—and his defeat of the Red Thief!"

I patted Zar on the head as everyone cheered.

"Pei do dna!" the Count added. "Bottoms up!"

To that, everyone clinked glasses and drank to the bottom. More bottles were opened and poured. I was not in the mood to celebrate. It felt wrong not to be under Papa's wing. I bid good night to Ruslan and was searching for Mama when Alexander appeared.

"May I steal you away for a moment?" he asked.

Zar and I followed him into the Count's library shelved in books from floor to ceiling along each of the four walls.

"It's you who deserve the credit," he said.

I braved to meet his eyes. They were like an ocean of blue—so vast, yet far from my world.

We clinked glasses and he toasted, "To my crystal ball!"

I blushed as I took a small sip.

"How is it that you always know where to be?" Alexander pressed. "I'm sure it wasn't a coincidence that you hid yourself on the sledge or sat with Zola the night of her birth. And there are so many other times I could list."

"Luck, I suppose." I couldn't tell him the truth, as much as I wanted to, as much as I *had* always wanted to tell him over the years.

"Then I wish I had your luck," he said.

Be careful what you wish for, I thought. To carry a gift like mine brings its own burdens.

"It's your turn to make a toast." The way Alexander looked at me made me feel like a treasured friend spun from sugar.

"J'aime ces chiens plus que tout." It was the first thing that came to me.

"That's not a toast," Alexander said. "Try again."

I looked down at Zar for inspiration. His trusting eyes made me smile. When I thought of Papa's Rules and how they interfered with my dream of breeding borzoi worthy of the Tsar, my smile faded. And when I thought of my future as a dressmaker . . . and Papa's wish to marry me off to the midwife's nephew . . . it all seemed . . . so hopeless . . . and that was when the words for my toast came to me.

"To the hope of hopeless matters!"

"To the hope of hopeless matters!" Alexander repeated.

We clinked glasses and drank until not a single drop of champagne remained.

"With the pressure of joining Father at the bell foundry looming over me, your toast couldn't say it any better," Alexander said.

Just then, chants for Zar echoed, growing louder and louder.

"We should go. They want Zar," I said.

The Count motioned for us to join him when we re-entered the ballroom. In one hand he held an unopened telegram high above his head. He positioned Alexander to his left and me to his right with Zar. I looked to Papa and his face was hard and still, like a stone embedded at the bottom of a river. As much as I willed them to, his eyes wouldn't meet mine.

"Does everyone have a full glass?" the Count asked.

Some hands were raised among the crowd and servers quickly attended to them. The Count cleared his throat. "It's not every day that a kennel discovers a gem as fine as Zar among the bunch. He represents what every kennel strives for: courage, strength, speed, and exceptional pluck."

I looked down at Zar and stroked his head. Papa would have no choice but to make him the top stud dog. Life on the estate would be different for Zar.

"It takes generations of careful breeding to develop a line of dogs worthy enough for the Tsar." The Count raised his glass high. "That's why I've decided to pass the kennel down to my son. It has been his dream to make something of this kennel, and he's done so—with help, of course—through the successful breeding of Zar. Let's toast to my son's future success!"

After Alexander clinked glasses with his father, he clinked glasses with me. "Thank you, Lara. We owe you a great deal of gratitude."

"Your dream is coming true," I said to him.

The Count patted Zar on the head and continued. "What I saw in Zar in the hunt for the Red Thief is nothing we can train a dog to do. What Zar has comes from deep within him. And despite his smaller size, and maybe because of it, too, Zar uses it to his advantage. He is agile and quick. He is courageous and clever. His pluck is peerless. Because of all these sound traits, I feel it isn't fair to hoard him to ourselves."

The Count rested his hand on my shoulder. "We have a fine litter from Zar to carry on his line. That's why

I've offered to present Zar to His Imperial Majesty Tsar Nicholas . . . and in this telegram, which has just arrived, I suspect is his response."

As the Count opened the telegram, I looked to Alexander, wondering if he knew about this. From the gape of his mouth he seemed just as shocked as I felt. Then I looked to Papa, and I could see that he, too, hung on every word. I searched for Mama in the crowd and found her warm amber eyes, willing me to be strong.

The Count's face blossomed into a huge smile as he read the words. "The Tsar has accepted!"

My crystal flute slipped from my hand and crashed to the floor. "Forgive me," I kept saying. Servers appeared and swept up the shards of glass all around me. I stood motionless, rooted to the ground, like a dead tree refusing to fall.

The Count glanced over at me with a puzzled look. Once another glass of champagne was in my hand, he continued with his toast. "Let's drink to our success," he proposed. He nodded to Papa first, and then to Alexander—whose mouth was still agape—and lastly to me. He even nodded to Zar.

I watched everyone around me drink and tried to raise my glass to my lips. But my fingers felt like wet noodles—and I dropped that flute, too.

CHAPTER FOURTEEN

The Dance

That night I escaped to the stable and found an empty stall in the birthing room. I didn't have energy to greet Zola and her pups, nor play with Chara. Instead, I laid a plush bear hide down on the soft, fresh straw and snuggled into it with Zar close to me. I wanted this night to end and hoped tomorrow would bring something different.

I woke the next morning, clinging to Zar like ivy, as Papa gently rustled me awake.

"I knew I'd find you here," Papa said. "It's where I used to come when I was troubled. Your mama was worried sick about you. I figured you needed this time with Zar and told her so. We're more alike than I knew, Larochka."

His words brought me comfort, as if I finally walked

along the same narrow trail with him through a dense forest, rather than through the thick of it all alone.

"It's time for Zar to make his journey," Papa said. "It's painful to let go of the dogs we love most. But this is what we do."

Papa took my hand and led me through the stable. Memories of Zar stirred inside me at every turn—his first lead, his first feed bowl, his mother, and his pups. I couldn't imagine walking through the stable without Zar. There were still too many memories we needed to build. I looked down at him prancing alongside me, as if today were like any other day—his eyes as trusting as ever.

Boris had the Count's finest horses hitched and ready to go. In the back of the sledge stood the wolf cage in which Zar would travel. Tinsel hung from the top of the cage to keep him safe from the forest spirits along the journey.

Alexander stood by the sledge and slowly walked over to me. "I'm so sorry, Lara."

"It was my dream, too—to breed borzoi worthy of the Tsar," I said.

Alexander looked like he wanted to say something more, but held his tongue.

"The Count left early this morning for the Tsar's palace," Papa said. "Say your goodbyes to Zar, and then Boris must be off to join him."

I bent down and hugged Zar. In his ear, I whispered, "The Tsar will give you much more than I ever could. You'll get the best training, the best meat, and the best home a dog could ever want. Be good for him, but most of all, continue to make us proud." I wiped back tears, and nodded to Papa that I was done saying my goodbyes.

"Have you forgotten something?" Papa pointed to the red ribbon I had tied around Zar's neck last night.

"I want him to have it," I answered. "So he won't forget me."

Papa's eyes started to water.

I led Zar to the sledge and into the wolf cage. He followed willingly and let me lock the cage. It wasn't until I jumped down from the sledge that Zar's feet started to dance in an effort to find a way out.

"Stay, Zar. Be a good dog," I said.

Zar tilted his head from one side to the next. I fought back my tears. I didn't want Papa or Alexander to think of me as a child. Boris clucked his tongue and the horses set off in a trot toward the gates of the estate with Zar caged up like a wolf in the back of the sledge. How Zar whined and yelped, and the way he gnawed and pawed at the wood slats of the cage to free himself made me wish it were me inside that horrible cage instead of him.

Pushkin's words came to me as my eyes followed Zar until he became a speck against the horizon.

Once again there hang beclouded
My horizons, dark with rain;
Envious Fate, in malice shrouded,
Lies in wait for me again.

Be careful what you wish for, I kept thinking. I had
certainly gotten what I had wished for. I just never realized how much it would hurt.

Papa rested his hands on my shoulders. "I need to talk
to you."

"Please, *Tyatya*. Not now."

"Yes, now," he said. "You'll want to hear what I should
have told you long ago—when you had your first vision."

An understanding warmth had crept into Papa's voice
as he took my hand. Because I blamed Papa for my mis-
ery, I expected my whole body to stiffen from his touch,
but it softened. In silence, I let him lead me past the kennel, past the main animal hospital, past the stable, past
the racetrack and show ring, past the wooden chapel and
its bell tower, past the birches, and past our home, into
the snowy fields under a cold blue sky. We stopped at the
river's edge, now frozen.

"I owe you the secret behind Golden Rule Number
Eight." Papa twisted the long, dark hairs of his beard
before the next words finally came. "Only a fool makes a
decision based on a vision."

At first I thought Papa was teasing me, then realized

from the pained look on his face, he had dug deep within himself to reveal this to me.

"Through the years all of the kennel stewards have had visions and learned to keep them a secret for fear of the harm they could bring upon us, as well as the bad choices we've made because of them."

Papa paused.

"What bad choices?" I asked.

"Long before you were born, something terrible happened," Papa admitted. "Your great-great-great-grandfather convinced the Count at the time to take the dogs on a hunt in the heart of a blizzard because he had had a vision of the dogs bringing down more wolves than on any other hunt. Though the Count had his doubts, he was eager to build the reputation of his kennel and trusted him. Together they went out in the snowy madness. One by one they lost the dogs. They would have died themselves had it not been for the pealing of the stable bells to guide them home."

"That's horrible, *Tyatya*."

"The Count in that day was so furious, he threatened to banish our family from the dogs. Because his wife was exceptionally fond of your great-great-great-grandmother, she persuaded her husband to give our family another chance on the condition that we never use our visions again."

"*Never?*" I asked.

"Never," Papa answered.

"Does Alexander know about this?" This would explain why he called me his crystal ball.

"Unlikely," Papa said. "It's nothing I've ever discussed with the Count."

"Why didn't you tell me all of this sooner?"

Papa rubbed his hand over his face. "I should have told you, but I felt a need to protect you, Larochka. People with gifts like ours come to be hated. Look at Rasputin. He won't live a long life, of this I'm certain."

"Our gift could be used to bring good, too," I said.

"I see that now." Papa sighed. "Your mama told me that you had wanted to warn me about the hunt. I was too thickheaded to listen and now I regret that choice. And as for Zar—you were right, it was good to let him live. These words have haunted me ever since his birth when you first said them. I knew you were right then and yet I refused to accept them. I didn't want you to have visions. Zar deserves much more credit than I've given to him. I just couldn't admit it to myself, until I faced the truth like a Cossack stallion headed for battle."

Just then, my head began to pound. Something in the pain I felt made me fear for Zar. I quickly squeezed my eyes shut and willed myself to see what was coming.

There behind my eyelids I saw Zar, hanging from a hunter's trap, swaying in the wind, above a pack of hungry wolves, jumping up at him with snarling, snapping jaws.

And then the image faded.

It left me with a cold, dark feeling that pressed on me until I could hardly breathe.

"I know that look," Papa said. "What did you see?"

"Zar's in danger," I murmured, swallowing back sobs.

"How can that be?"

"I don't know. He must have freed himself—"

Papa cut me off. "That's impossible. I made that cage myself."

"I know what I saw." I folded my arms and stood a little taller. "Zar's hanging from a tree, stuck in a hunter's loop. If we don't find him soon, I'm afraid the wolves will."

Papa stroked the long, dark hairs of his beard in pensive thought. "I know of one hunter who uses loops to trap wolves."

"We need him to show us where his traps are," I said.

Just then, our stable bells rang in earnest—*ding-ding-ding-ding*—in a call for help. Papa and I hurried to the stable and found that Boris had returned. He paced back and forth, pointing to the empty cage, as Alexander listened and watched.

"What happened?" Papa asked Boris as we approached full out of breath.

"One minute I looked back and Zar was inside the cage, in the next he was gone. He somehow managed to push the latch free," Boris said. "I returned to the estate hoping to find him here."

"We've searched the kennel. We didn't find him," Alexander said, giving me a look that said he shared my pain.

"Because he hasn't yet made it home," Papa said. He turned to me. "Go ahead, explain, Lara. I give you my blessing."

As afraid as I was of being hated like Rasputin, I couldn't let anything happen to Zar. So I closed my eyes. I couldn't bear to see how Alexander would react when he learned of my visions.

"Zar's hanging from a hunter's loop, trapped above a hungry pack of wolves," I blurted.

Nobody spoke.

In the silence, I braved to open one of my eyes.

Papa stood tall and self-assured.

Alexander's face was full of questions.

To my surprise, Boris, bullish and brawny, took a step back, staring wide-eyed at me. He looked ready to run, like a frightened hare.

"I know it sounds far-fetched, but I believe her," Papa said.

"I don't understand," Alexander said.

"I have visions," I answered in a soft voice. "I see things before they happen."

"How?" Alexander asked.

"I don't know. They come and go with no real pattern other than they're connected to the dogs."

"Is that why you're always in the right place at the right time?" Alexander asked.

I nodded.

"It's starting to make sense," Alexander said. "There had been rumors, but I pushed them aside as myth. I wish I had paid more attention to them."

From the pleased tone of Alexander's voice I allowed myself to breathe again. "You don't hate me?"

"Not if it helps us save Zar," he said. "Why didn't you tell me?"

"It's my fault," Papa said. "I made her promise not to tell anyone."

"It killed me not to tell you," I said to Alexander. "There were so many times that I wanted to."

"Keeping your word is admirable," Alexander said. "You're more noble than you think."

"We must hurry, Alexander. Papa knows of a hunter who uses traps like the one I saw. We need him to show us where he's set them up. In one of them, I'm certain that we'll find Zar."

"Boris, we'll need a bigger sleigh and a fresh set of horses," Alexander requested.

"Right away." Boris hustled inside the stable, looking over his shoulder, eyeing me as if I were a wolf cub in a pen filled with chicks.

Alexander, Papa, and I rode through the powdery snow some twenty versts away to a small log house in the deep, dark woods.

The hunter was chopping wood outside. Alexander and Papa exchanged a few words with him, and then Alexander handed the hunter a bag of rubles. They shook hands and soon we were headed through the woods again with the hunter leading the way on his own sledge.

"The first one's up ahead," the hunter said. It had not yet been triggered.

We traveled to the next one, and again it was empty. So was the third trap.

"You sure your dog might be in one of my traps?" the hunter asked. He lifted his bag of coins and jingled it. "Seems you wasted this on nothing."

"How many more traps do you have?" Papa asked. "We want to see all of them."

"The others are further away."

Alexander looked at me. "Lara?"

"Yes, all of them."

Day was becoming night. We could not travel as quickly through the woods under the darkening sky. I pulled the small black box that Ruslan had made from my pocket and fingered Zar's face.

Then I kissed his face three times, just as Mama did in times of hope.

"Up ahead," the hunter directed Papa.

There in the trap was something white. It lay motion-less, as if already dead. My heart dropped into the pit of my stomach. "Zar?"

As we approached the trap, my heartbeat slowed. It was a silver-white wolf.

"Let me cut that wolf down!" the hunter shouted.

"We don't have time," Papa said. "It's urgent we find our dog."

Alexander turned to me. "Can you remember any-thing else from your vision?"

I closed my eyes and tried to recall what I had seen. "Birch trees! I saw birch trees."

I called out to the hunter. "Do you have a trap set among a cluster of birch trees?"

"Yes, I do." The hunter gulped. "How did you know that?"

"Bring us to it," I said. "There we'll find our dog."

"Just over that hill." The hunter pointed. "Do you see those birches in the distance?"

Papa cracked the knout and the horses picked up speed. I thought I could hear Zar's barking in the distance—his cries for help. As we got closer, my heart hammered and my body started to shake. I kept telling myself to take deep breaths, but my throat tightened and I could hardly breathe.

"That isn't just any dog," the hunter said. "That's a borzoi!"

There under the birches hung Zar, caught in a trap, trying to free himself above a pack of hungry wolves.

"Hold on, Zar!" I called.

Alexander pulled out his rifle and shot into the pack that hovered under Zar. One wolf dropped and some scattered.

He reloaded and shot again at the pack. Another wolf crumpled into the snow and more wolves bolted in fear.

Papa drove the sleigh just underneath Zar. The hunter dismounted from his sledge and lowered Zar into the sleigh and into my arms—arms I wrapped around Zar. Arms I didn't want to let go. I stroked Zar's head, half laughing, half crying, waiting for my heartbeat to calm, my shaking to stop. Zar licked my ears and gave them little bites of affection, grunting with pure delight. And he wouldn't stop. He kept giving me little bites, like all his love was stored up in them. I retrieved my lucky knife and cut Zar free from the rope.

"Zar belongs with you," Alexander said to me. "That's clear."

"For once I have to agree," Papa said.

I cupped Zar's ears. "*Nyet,* he has to go to the Tsar. A promise is a promise."

It killed me to say these words aloud.

"Are you sure, Larochka?" Papa asked.

"Alexander's family would lose favor with the Tsar if we don't," I said.

"Not if we send His Imperial Majesty pups from Zar's litter," Alexander proposed. "What would be better than a troika of his progeny?"

Alexander's idea was tempting. I sure would prefer to keep Zar at my side. But it also went against my dream to breed borzoi worthy of the Tsar.

"I can't let you make that mistake, Alexander. Your family needs to send Zar. He's your best dog and it's the best thing to do for the Woronzova Kennel," I said. "Also, what will your father tell His Imperial Majesty Tsar Nicholas if Zar doesn't show up?"

Alexander turned to my papa.

"This is your decision," Papa said. "Though I agree with Lara, sending Zar to the Tsar is the best choice for the kennel."

"We'll still have Zar's pups to carry his line," I said. Then I held him tightly around his neck, giving *him* small bites of affection. I took a deep breath, garnered all my strength, and whispered into Zar's ear, "You must carry on the Woronzova line and make us all proud." Zar tilted his head and nudged my chin. "I'll never forget you, Zar."

"All right, then it's settled," Alexander said. "Zar goes in the morning."

The hunter collected the dead wolves and loaded them onto his sledge. We thanked him and parted ways.

Along our journey home I held Zar close in my lap.

Alexander leaned into me. "It's very brave of you to give up Zar. I know how much he means to you."

"It's the right thing to do, Sasha," I said.

"Still, I'll never forget what you did for my family."

When we were a few versts away from the estate, Papa lifted his hunting horn from his neck and handed it to me.

It felt heavy with memories—memories from past stewards who wore the horn around their necks, too. I traced the outline of the gold borzoi running with outstretched legs, as Zar nosed it with his long snout. "This is you."

Zar tilted his head from side to side, and then pawed at the horn.

"Gentle, boy." I lifted the horn away from his long legs, over my head, and around my neck.

"Go ahead, Lara. Let Boris, Maxim, and the rest of the kennel hands know we're coming with good news," Papa said.

"Really?" I asked.

"You've earned it, Lara."

I brought the horn to my lips, took a deep breath, and blew as hard and as long as I could.

Alexander clapped. *"Molodietz!"*

I looked to Papa and he patted my head as he would with one of the dogs. It had been a long time since he had done that—and a long time since I had felt as one with him.

I removed the horn from my neck and handed it back to Papa.

Papa put up his hands. "It's yours now."

"Does this mean—"

Papa raised his finger high in the air, as if he were the Tsar. "As the current Woronzova Kennel steward, and by the power vested in me by my forefathers, it's obvious you belong with the dogs."

I made Papa repeat these words several times before I finally believed him. And then I asked, "What about the midwife's nephew?"

"I understand he's afraid of dogs," Papa said, winking at Alexander. "I doubt he'd be a suitable match for my daughter."

I turned to Alexander and hugged him for being such a loyal friend.

"And until I do find a suitable match on whom we can both agree," Papa added, "I'll be expecting solid results from you with Zar's pups."

"Oh, *Tyatya!*" My heart hammered as though it would burst between my rib cage, and my head filled up with plans to breed Chara as soon as possible to ensure Zar's lineage. "I promise not to disappoint you."

Papa pulled a flask out from the inside pocket of his

Cossack jacket, patched and frayed. "In the spirit of Golden Rule Number Two—hope for the best, prepare for the worst." He took a swill from the flask, and then passed it to Alexander.

Alexander raised the flask and nodded his head to me. "Here's to selfishly keeping you on the estate to build my dream."

When he handed me the flask, I put it to my lips and took a sip, just as they had done. As the plum brandy warmed my insides, I felt like I finally belonged.

"I'd like to propose a few changes, too," I said.

Papa eyed me with suspicion. "One change at a time, Lara."

I crossed my arms and Zar poked Papa with his long nose.

"She deserves an attentive ear," Alexander said.

"All right, all right," Papa said.

I cleared my throat and raised my finger high in the air, as if I were the Tsar. "As long as the future Count agrees, I hereby abolish Golden Rule Number Eight—visions shall no longer be shunned as evil. They'll be embraced for the gift they are and put to good use."

"That will take some getting used to," Papa said.

With an encouraging nod from Alexander, I continued. "As for your silly new Rule, Golden Rule Number Nine. It has to change." I looked down at Zar. "Anyone with a passion to hunt should be allowed to follow that passion."

"Let's toast to that," Alexander said.

Again, we passed the flask of plum brandy around.

I took a sip, and it suddenly dawned on me. "What about Bohdan, Papa?" It didn't seem right to rob him of becoming kennel steward.

"When he's old enough, we'll ask him if the dogs call to him," Papa answered. "Who knows? He might take after his mama and prefer a needle and thread."

"And if he doesn't?" I asked.

"I suppose we could have two kennel stewards," Papa answered, looking at Alexander for his reaction. "There's nothing in the Golden Rules against it."

"I'm all for it," Alexander said.

"Did you hear that, Zar?" I asked. "Papa said I could become the next kennel steward. I owe it all to you."

Zar gave Papa his paw and nudged his elbow.

"He wants to shake on it," I said.

Papa laughed and shook Zar's paw.

When we approached the estate, the stable bells rang like a chorus of singing icons, as if the Tsar was expected. Everyone from the kitchen staff to the stable hands hovered at the entrance of the stable doors—even Mama, rocking Bohdan in her arms. Next to her stood Ruslan, waving his arms frantically. Like at Christmastime, the mood was festive and the spirit was high. Papa pulled on the reins and the sleigh came to a stop. Everyone gathered around us, applauding our success.

I pulled out the black box decorated with Zar's image and raised it high over my head. "It brought us luck!"

"It's you who brought the luck," Ruslan said.

"He's right. Boris told us what happened." Mama gave me a teary-eyed wink and her wet cheeks glistened under the full moon. "I knew you'd find a way. I'm so proud of you. So is Bohdan. Listen to him coo."

Zar was first to jump out of the sleigh, his feathery tail wagging, his eyes watching my every move, his feet dancing from paw to paw—waiting for me to join him. No sooner did my feet land on the packed snow than Zar lifted his paw into my hand and then gingerly placed his other paw onto my shoulder. He stood a head or more taller than me. "Whoa, boy! What's this all about?"

"Zar wants to dance," Alexander encouraged.

"He sure does," Ruslan added.

In mirth and wonder, as if I just touched the moon, I twirled Zar around in a fancy waltz. With his long snout he nudged underneath the earflaps of my fur hat and gave my ears tiny bites of affection. Mama and Bohdan joined us—as did Papa with his bear-hug arms wrapped around all of us.

AUTHOR'S NOTE

My first visit to Russia was as a student in 1984 during the Cold War era, shortly before Mikhail Gorbachev became the Soviet premier of the USSR. I am not of Russian descent, but I became fascinated by the Russian culture, people, and arts. I knew I wanted to go back to Russia in some capacity to help foster the relationship between our countries. So I got an MBA in international business, studied the Russian language, and off I went back to Russia in 1989 to work as a consultant for a newly formed Soviet co-op, similar to what we in the United States call a small business.

Because I love dogs, and with the responsibilities of school behind me, I decided to get a Russian dog and opted for a borzoi, what I considered a true Russian breed. I thought I would find plenty of borzoi in the homeland, but that wasn't the case. Through my struggle finding Dasha, a borzoi pup, I learned the history of Russia. I knew there was a story behind my experience, and that's when the seed was first planted for *Lara's Gift*.

My story idea grew when I met Bonnie Dalzell, an American Kennel Club borzoi judge and breeder, at a coursing event. She gave me a copy of a book called *Observations on Borzoi,* about the early 1900s travels of a wealthy American, Joseph B. Thomas, and his quest for the perfect borzoi in Russia. He declared the top three Russian borzoi kennels as those belonging to Tsar Nicholas, the Grand Duke Nicolai, and Count Vorontsov. I didn't think much of it at first, until I bumped into Professor Alexander Woronzoff-Dashkoff, from my days at Smith College studying Russian. He admired Dasha and commented that his great-great-great-uncle used to breed borzoi. And then it clicked. The family names of Woronzoff and Vorontsov were one and the same. I had a million questions for Professor Woronzoff, but it was the questions he couldn't answer and all the "what-ifs" that made my story idea take off.

There are some things I need to note for you along your reading journey. For the record, the plural of *borzoi* is *borzoi* and I have honored this. In my research of Count Vorontsov's famous borzoi kennel, it was commonly cited in my English sources as Woronzova Kennel, with an *a* at the end, which most likely reflected the pronunciation to an American ear. However, if translated properly from Russian to English, it probably should have been referred to as Woronzovo Kennel, with an *o* at the end. In this case, I have used the former spelling, which is what is most often cited in borzoi history sources. I have done my best to accurately portray this time period in history down to the tiniest of details. Although I take full responsibility for any inaccuracies, I have taken some liberties that I have addressed below.

In Russia, it is customary for Russians to address each other using their full name, including their patronymic name, which originates from the father's first name. Only when Russians are on very familiar terms do they address each other by their first name alone. For the purpose of this story, I have omitted the patronymic name and have used either the first name or the family name to refer to each character. The Russian names I use in the book are those of actual people who lived and worked on the Vorontsov estate in the mid-1800s that I found in a census record.

During the Imperial Era, peasant girls called their fathers *Tyatya*, which translates to "Daddy" in English. They would not have called their father Papa. This title was reserved for nobility. Whenever Lara addresses her father in speech, I correctly use the term *Tyatya*. However, to keep things simple, I have used Papa instead of Father throughout to create the kind of tone I wanted for this story. The same scenario applies to Mama. Wherever Lara addresses her mama directly in dialogue, I have used the correct term of *Matushka*.

Borzoi pups were named by their owners after famous borzoi and from a short list of traditional names. They were not necessarily named by the kennel steward's daughter. In my story, given Lara's gift and her special relationship with Alexander, I feel it's plausible that she would have been given the honor. For the most part, the names she did give the pups are names that would have been given at the time this story takes place, with the exception of Ryczar, which means "knight." An uneducated peasant girl might not have known this word. However, because of her love for Pushkin, I believe a girl like Lara may have been familiar with this word. Because she wants to honor Zar's mother, Zarya, and because she's not educated, she shortens it incorrectly to "Zar" instead of "Czar."

Because Pushkin's poems are so lyrical, I believe it's plausible that a girl like Lara could have memorized some of her favorite stanzas. Many of Pushkin's fairy tales were shared in an oral fashion and passed down from one generation to the next in this manner as well.

Although girls Lara's age with her social status during the Imperial Era wore colorful scarves over their heads, I chose to give Lara a fur hat because this is how I saw her character.

During the Imperial Era, Russians were known worldwide for the quality of the bells they produced for the church. Russian Orthodox Christians, whether working in the fields during harvesttime or standing inside a church, would listen to the ringing of the bells to follow the various stages of the mass. Because there was an abundance of bells made by the fictional Count Vorontsov's bell foundry, and because of his kennel's long history, I have stretched the purpose of the bells beyond their traditional use in the church to serve elsewhere on the grand estate—such as for hunts, births, and finding one's way home through a snowy blizzard.

At the time my story takes place, only nobility could own borzoi. These dogs were also never sold for money. They were given to friends, often other nobles abroad, as gifts. If a non-noble stole a borzoi or was caught with one, the punishment was severe. Although Lara saves Zar from being culled and treats him as her own, she is fully aware that Zar is the property of the Count.

Although it was not common for a Russian noble to marry or befriend someone beneath their social status, I found enough examples in my research to move forward with the friendship that Alexander and Lara share. Often, these grand estates were isolated from other estates and far from city life, making it convenient for the children of some peasants and nobles to become playmates.

In my research, I also found many examples of abusive husbands, submissive wives, and obedient children among Russian peasant families. I like to think that not all peasant families were like this. Surely, there were exceptions. Nevertheless, I may have taken liberties by giving Lara some pluck and a strong will to work with the borzoi, as well as with her *Matushka,* by giving her a voice to express her opinions. I kept with tradition, however, in maintaining the father's role in finding a husband for his daughter.

Dogs were and are not allowed inside a Russian church. Although Lara is fully aware of this and for the most part respectful of the church and its establishment, her love of Zar is so strong, she breaks this well-known rule.

Russians have a rich culture of offering toasts and will often find any reason to celebrate. It is part of their everyday life and is accurately represented throughout *Lara's Gift.*

Over the last hundred years, most wolf attacks on humans have involved individual wolves and have been extremely rare. I have taken some liberties in the climax of *Lara's Gift* in order to create good fiction. It's important to note that the wolf has historically been a controversial animal because of livestock losses and human safety, which led to attempts at extermination of wolves around the world. Modern environmental protections and conservation initiatives have supported wolf recovery—

many with great success. Today, the biggest threat to wolves is our own human belief systems. How we view the wolf as a large predator through the lens of our own value systems will influence whether or not we will allow wolves to exist into the future. Additionally, how we use the landscape for our own purposes will directly affect whether wolves have a place to exist.

Before you rush out to get a borzoi pup, please do your research to determine if this breed of dog is the right match for your situation. The borzoi is considered a giant breed, with an average height of 28 to 32 inches and an average weight of 60 to 100 pounds. They require exercise and should never be let off a leash in an unfenced area. They are an intelligent and affectionate breed, but are independent and can be stubborn. Borzoi come in a wide variety of colors besides white, cream, gold, and champagne. For a list of standard AKC colors, please see Bonnie Dalzell's list at borzoi-color.batw.net/quick_color.html. One of my favorite borzoi colors is black. Borzoi are not like most popular breeds of dogs. For more detailed information, please go to borzoiclubofamerica.org.

In borrowing from Kathi Appelt's wise words of comfort to her animal-loving readers of *The Underneath*, I want to assure my readers that there were no animals harmed or injured in the writing of *Lara's Gift*.

A portion of the proceeds from the sale of *Lara's Gift* will be donated to the National Borzoi Rescue

Foundation (nbrf.org) to ensure that all borzoi in need find a forever home, and to the International Wolf Center (wolf.org) to advance the survival of wolf populations by teaching about wolves, their relationship to wild lands, and the role of humans in their future.

AFTERWORD

Artemii Vorontsov (Woronzoff), my great-great-great-uncle, loved his daughter Praskovia so much that in her dowry he included Vorontsova (Woronzova), a family estate in the province of Tambov, in central Russia. It was a beautiful place with a tree-lined entrance leading to a large, two-story house. Situated on the high banks of the Tsna River, it was surrounded by a large park with cascading ponds leading to the river below. The estate comprised the stone manor house, a church, outbuildings, greenhouses, stables, the kennels, and other dependencies.

Praskovia gave the estate to her daughter Elizabeth, and it was Elizabeth's son, Artemii Boldyrev (named for his great-grandfather Artemii Vorontsov), who bred at Vorontsova the famous line of magnificent white borzoi.

Artemii's wife, Maria, also took a keen interest in the dogs. She was an excellent horsewoman and often participated in the hunt.

Today, only the park remains. The estate has disappeared and so have its owners, victims of revolutions, wars, and the great political and social changes in Russia during the twentieth century. A small museum in the neighboring village of Vorontsovka preserves the memory of the families and dogs that once lived there.

In *Lara's Gift*, Annemarie O'Brien also preserves the past by submerging us in a time and place that is now gone but that holds us captive by its beauty and elegance, as well as its contradictions and inequalities. She vividly reconstructs everyday estate life—the echoes of distant church bells, the sounding of the horn, the stark cruelty of the hunt, and the joys and pain of birth. But most of all, she presents us with a young girl's strength, perseverance, and enduring love for her dog.

Alexander Woronzoff-Dashkoff
Professor of Russian
Smith College

GLOSSARY

All foreign words are in Russian unless otherwise noted.

ALMAZ: Diamond
BABOCHKA: Butterfly
BABUSHKA: Grandmother
BISTRI: Quick
BLINI: Russian pancakes
BOHDAN: Russian name for a male meaning "gift from God"
BOLSHOE SPASIBO: A big thanks
BOREI: North wind
BORSCHT: Beet and cabbage soup
BRONYA: Armor
BURAN: Snowstorm

BUYAN: Rebel

CHAI: Tea

CHARA: Charm, enchantment

CHONG RAHMAT: Kyrgyz for "a big thanks"

DAVAI!: Come on! Let's go!

DOBRAYA: Kind

DOROGAYA: Good one

DOROGUSHA: Very good one

GOSPODI: Oh my God

J'AIME CES CHIENS PLUS QUE TOUT: French for "I love these dogs more than anything."

KASHA: Porridge

KNOUT: A whip with a lash of leather thongs

KOPECK: Russian form of currency in which 100 kopecks amounts to 1 ruble

KOROTYSHKA: Runt

LAROCHKA: A diminutive form of Lara, which comes from the name Larissa and means "protection"

LOVKIY: Expert

MAHALO: Hawaiian for "thank you"

MATUSHKA: Mommy, the term a peasant girl like Lara would use to address her mother

MOLODIETZ!: Good job!

NYET: No

OCHEN BOLSHOE SPASIBO: A big thanks

OI: Ouch

PEI DO DNA!: Bottoms up!

POZHALUISTA: Please

RADUGA: Rainbow

RASPUTIN: Grigori Yefimovich Rasputin (1869–1916) was a Russian mystic who was suspected of having undue influence over the last Tsar, Nicholas II; his wife, Alexandra; and their only son, Alexei. There is much controversy over Rasputin. He was called a "psychic" and the "Mad Monk," a *"strannik"* (religious pilgrim) and even a *"starets"* (elder). The royal family brought him into their circle to help them heal their son, Alexei, who had hemophilia. It has been argued that Rasputin helped to discredit the Tsarist government, leading to the fall of the Romanov dynasty in 1917. He was sent into and out of exile from 1909 until his death.

ROSSAK: Gray hare

RUBLE: The basic monetary unit of Russia, equal to 100 kopecks

RYCZAR: Knight

RYSS: Lynx

SASHA: A diminutive form of Alexander

SEMPER IMMOTA FIDES: Latin for "Always Steadfast Loyalty"

SHAIKA: Bandit tribe

SILA: Force

SKORAYA: Rapid

SNIGURKA: Snow maiden

SOSKA: Baby pacifier made of rags

SPASIBO: Thank you

TARAN: Battering ram

TYATYA: Daddy, the term a peasant girl like Lara would use to address her father

UMNITZA: Clever one

VERST: One verst equals 0.66 miles or 1.067 kilometers

VLAST: Power

VOLAN: Kite

ZANOZA: Splinter, thorn in one's flesh, sweetheart (also the name of one of Alfred A. Knopf's borzoi)

ZAR: Lara's diminutive form of the Russian word *ryczar*, which means "knight"

ZARYA: Dawn

ZOLA: A diminutive form of the Russian word *zolotaya*, which means "golden"

ZVEZDA: Star

ZVON: Russian term for a set of tower bells in the Orthodox Church that are rung liturgically and on various festive occasions by manually pulling ropes attached to inside clappers. Could loosely be translated as "chime" or "peal" as well.

BIBLIOGRAPHY

Afanasiev, Alexander. *The Magic Ring: Russian Folk Tales.* Illustrated by A. Kurkin. Moscow: Raduga, 1978.

Baedeker, Karl. *Russia: Handbook for Travelers.* Leipzig: Karl Baedeker, 1914.

The Borzoi: The Dog Anthology. Warwickshire, UK: Vintage Dog Books, 2007.

Bucher, Greta. *Daily Life in Imperial Russia.* Westport, CT: Greenwood Press, 2008.

Chadwick, Winifred. *The Borzoi Handbook.* London: Love & Malcomson, 1952.

Dashkova, Ekaterina Romanovna. *The Memoirs of Princess Dashkova.* Durham, NC: Duke University Press Books, 1995.

Goldstein, Darra. *A Taste of Russia*. New York: HarperPerennial, 1991.

Grosvenor, Gilbert H. "Young Russia: The Land of Unlimited Possibilities." *National Geographic* 26.5, November 1914, 423–520. Print.

Kirk, R. G. *Zanoza*. Illustrated by Harvey Dunn. New York: Alfred A. Knopf, 1918.

Lincoln, W. Bruce. *Sunlight at Midnight: St. Petersburg and the Rise of Modern Russia*. New York: Basic Books, 2002.

Massie, Suzanne. *Land of the Firebird: The Beauty of Old Russia*. Blue Hill, ME: Heart Tree Press, 1980.

Nabokov, Vladimir. *Mary*. New York: Vintage International, 1989.

———. *Speak, Memory*. New York: Vintage International, 1989.

Nikitenko, Aleksandr. *Up from Serfdom: My Childhood and Youth in Russia, 1804–1824*. Translated by Helen Saltz Jacobson. New Haven, CT: Yale University Press, 2001.

The Peasant in Nineteenth-Century Russia. Edited by Wayne S. Vucinich. Stanford, CA: Stanford University Press, 1968.

Pushkin, Alexander. *Collected Narrative and Lyrical Poetry*. Translated and edited by Walter Arndt. Dana Point, CA: Ardis, 1984.

———. "Count Nulin." *Cardinal Points Literary Journal*. Translated by Betsy Hulick. New York: Stosvet Press, July 2011. 3:112. Print.

Roosevelt, Priscilla. *Life on the Russian Country Estate.* New Haven, CT: Yale University Press, 1995.

Russian Peasant Women. Edited by Beatrice Farnsworth and Lynne Viola. New York: Oxford University Press, 1992.

Semyonova Tian-Shanskaia, Olga. *Village Life in Late Tsarist Russia.* Edited by David L. Ransel. Bloomington: Indiana University Press, 1993.

Thomas, Joseph B. *Observations on Borzoi.* Boston: Houghton Mifflin Company, 1912.

Troyat, Henri. *Daily Life in Russia Under the Last Tsar.* Stanford, CA: Stanford University Press, 1979.

Vyrubova, Anna. "Memories of the Russian Court." alexander palace.org/russiancourt/l.html. Retrieved September 2, 2009. Web.

Waldron, Peter. *The End of Imperial Russia, 1855–1917.* New York: Palgrave Macmillan, 1997.

Windle, Joy E. *Being Borzoi.* Coatesville, PA: Zoistory, 2007.

———. *Forever Borzoi.* Coatesville, PA: Zoistory, 2008.

Woronzoff-Dashkoff, Alexander. *Dashkova: A Life of Influence and Exile.* Philadelphia: American Philosophical Society, 2008.

Worthing, Eileen. *The Life & Legends of the Borzoi.* Illustrated by Teri Bednarczyk. Wheat Ridge, CO: Donald R. Hoflin, 1977.

Youssoupoff, Prince Felix. *Lost Splendor.* New York: Helen Marx Books, 2003.

Zerebko, Irene. *Russian Names for Russian Dogs.* Fairfax, VA: Denlinger's Publishers, 1985.

ACKNOWLEDGMENTS

There are many people I want to thank for opening gilded doors along my path of discovering borzoi, the craft of writing, Russia, and the world beyond. Hanne Burns and Alice Clemente, my childhood neighbors, fed my curiosity about the world and instilled in me an early desire to travel to new places. I give my biggest teddy bear hug to the late Igor Zelljadt, for teaching me Russian at Smith College.

I owe Suzanne Stafford, one of the first American women to do business in the former USSR, a *bolshoe spasibo* for connecting me to my first job in Russia. Without Suzanne, I never would have met Igor Belov, Sergei Bugnui, Misha Petriga, Sergei Golubaev, or Yuri Nivitski. Together they helped me find my first authentic Russian borzoi pup, Dasha. Without them, this book would not exist, for the struggles we overcame inspired this story.

Bonnie Dalzell, owner of Silkenswift Borzoi Kennel and an AKC borzoi judge, fed further inspiration when she gifted me a book, *Observations on Borzoi* by Joseph B. Thomas, about his early 1900s travels to Russia in search of the perfect borzoi. When I saw photos of the Woronzova borzoi, it launched a thousand questions and wonderings. Thank you, Bonnie, for teaching me so much about borzoi.

When I began my writing career, I was fortunate to get excellent advice from Patricia MacLachlan, another childhood neighbor and the author of *Sarah, Plain and Tall*, a Newbery Medal winner. She was the first to suggest that I join SCBWI and get an MFA in Writing for Children and Young Adults from the Vermont College of Fine Arts. At VCFA I found my home away from home and worked with faculty advisors Uma Krishnaswami, Jane Kurtz, Marion Dane Bauer, and Cynthia Leitich Smith, as well as workshop leaders Rita Garcia-Williams, Shelley Tanaka, Sharon Darrow, Julie Larios, David Gifaldi, and Margaret Bechard. To all of you I give my warmest embrace. Hugs also go to the Cliffhangers, the Revisionistas, and the Super Secret Society of Quirk and Quill for welcoming me into each of their classes.

I also got full-novel critiques of this story from Carolyn Coman, M. T. Anderson, Nina Lindsay, and Deborah Halverson, who offered invaluable insight and asked just the right questions to help me through some trouble spots.

Another *bolshoe spasibo* goes to my writing group, Beyond the Margins: Ann Jacobus, Frances Lee Hall, Linden McNeilly, Christine Dowd, and Helen Pyne. They saw several drafts of *Lara's Gift* and shared constructive guidance that helped me shape this story. Other writing friends who deserve thanks include Jessica Powers, Emily Jiang, Mary Colgan, Abigail Samoun, Caroline Goodwin, and Caitlyn Berry. But it's Amanda Materne who deserves the tightest embrace and biggest box of chocolate for giving me spot-on critiques along my journey of writing *Lara's Gift*.

I also thank SCBWI founders Lin Oliver and Stephen Mooser, as well as those behind the scenes at SCBWI, for creating a community of such supportive people and the kind of resources that help new authors launch their writing careers. Through SCBWI I have made countless friends—Meg O'Hair, Connie Goldsmith, and Patti Newman, to name a few—and received constructive feedback along the way from professionals like Kendra Markus, Minju Chang, Anne Hoppe, and many others.

There aren't enough boxes of chocolate in the world to appropriately thank my friends and family who have never wavered in their support of me: the late Blair

Torrey, his parents, Jay and the late Dana Torrey, and family; Kathy Morrissey; Amy Myer; Waltraud and the late Walter Grupp; Cornelia Pankau and her family; Diana Grupp; Jacqueline Curzon; Angelia Barnes; Cameron Rinker and his family; Santosh and Kirsten Soren; Chris Allen; Sheila Driscoll Fleck; Amy O'Neil; Ann Young Zarider; Antonio Cavaliere; Willo Carey; Beverly Hagerdon Thakur and her lovely husband, Duni; Natalia and John Alsup; Alice Temple; Mary Johnston; Christina and Marshall Whitley and their children; Shawn Stout; Elyse Evans; Andrea Calderon Thomas; Christiane dos Santos; Paul Morrissey; and my sisters, Cathy Christensen and Nan Skeffington, and their families.

I thank my brother, Ted O'Brien, for timely acupuncture treatments and his belief in me; Jonathan Kalmakoff for help with my research of Russian names; Andrey Kneller for sharing his love of Pushkin; Betsy Hulick for her wonderful translation of "Count Nulin," Pushkin's poem that starts with a borzoi wolf hunt; Jess Edberg, from the International Wolf Center, for her knowledge of wolves; Roman Kozakand and Irina Petrova for their expertise on Russian traditional costumes; Tricia and Harry Joiner for their expertise on Palekh icons and art; and to *all* of my students, from whom I continue to grow as a writer.

For entrusting me with my borzoi Zola, I thank Sarah

Fry, as well as Garnett Thompson of Sunburst Kennel and Charlotte Ansbro Wheeler of the v'Indra Kennel. Zola is the sweetest and most vocal borzoi I have ever met. I thank Irene Carroll for entrusting me with Zar. He is every bit as loyal as the fictional Zar and the best dog I have ever had.

I thank Gabrielle Slater of Russkaya Borzoi in the United Kingdom for putting me in touch with Anna Mihalskaya, Russian borzoi expert, literature professor, and author of *The Breed*, who carefully read *Lara's Gift* for Russian language, borzoi facts, and historical accuracy. Her comments were immensely helpful.

I also extend endless thanks to Professor Alexander Woronzoff-Dashkoff for living up to his family's motto of steadfast loyalty, inscribed on the Vorontsov coat of arms, by honoring my story with the lovely afterword, and to his wife, Katia, who believed in *Lara's Gift*.

Chong rahmat to Talant Begaliev for encouraging me to take risks.

Rocky Ho deserves a big *mahalo* for selflessly being my rock.

I thank Sally and her husband, Ollie Seymour, contractor extraordinaire, for renovating my writing cottage, which sits in my garden among tall roses and offers me a peaceful and comfortable place to sink into Lara's world.

Special thanks go to the Greenhouse Literary Agency

and Sarah Davies, my lovely agent, for taking me on. Her style, work ethic, and knowledge of the industry are unparalleled.

Nancy Sondel gets boundless hugs for acting on my wish to invite Erin Clarke, editor at Knopf, to her YA Novel Workshop at PCCWW, where Erin first met Lara and Zar.

It is a dream come true that my book will carry the Knopf colophon of a borzoi along its spine and initial pages. It took the efforts of many people at Random House to bring my story to you. I thank Stephanie Moss for her lovely vision of the cover for *Lara's Gift* and Tim Jessell for his priceless execution. I'd also like to recognize and thank Ronnie Ambrose, Artie Bennett, Judy Kiviat, Karen Mugler, and Alison Kolani, the team of Random House copy editors who carefully pored over the pages of *Lara's Gift* with a keen borzoi eye, made many astute comments, and taught me a few good grammar lessons.

But it is Erin Clarke, my dream editor, whom I thank most of all, for taking *Lara's Gift* under her wing and giving it flight. She carefully read my manuscript and gave me clear direction to strengthen my story, leading me through the revision process with her spot-on advice, much like the pealing of bells guiding me home through a Russian blizzard.

An *ochen bolshoe spasibo* goes to the O'Brien and Mitchell families for being the best cast of characters a girl could ever want and need. There are far too many of you to name, but you know who you are! Thanks go to Richard for giving me an impenetrable coat of armor. Big, meaty bones go to the real Zola and Zar, who were often at my feet as I wrote. Most of all, I thank my parents for believing in me, and my children, Aubrey and Anjuli, for their patience when I needed to write and for the excitement they shared with me when they learned that *Lara's Gift* would be published by Knopf.

ABOUT THE AUTHOR

Annemarie O'Brien has an MFA from the Vermont College of Fine Arts in Writing for Children and Young Adults. She teaches courses in writing for children at UC Berkeley and Stanford and edits children's books for Room to Read, an organization that advocates literacy in developing countries. Annemarie spent many years living and working in Russia, where the inspiration for *Lara's Gift*, her debut novel, developed. She now lives in Northern California with her family; two borzoi dogs, Zola and Zar; and a silken windhound named Zeus.

For more information about the author, please go to annemarieobrienauthor.com.